JACKIE
MANTHORNE

GHOST MOTEL

gynergy
books

Cover illustration: Brenda Whiteway

Printed and bound in Canada by: Hignell Printing Ltd.

gynergy books acknowledges the generous support of the Canada Council.

Published by:
gynergy books
P.O. Box 2023
Charlottetown, P.E.I.
Canada, C1A 7N7

Distributors:
Canada: General Distribution Services
United States: Inland Book Company
United Kingdom: Turnaround Distribution

Canadian Cataloguing in Publication Data
Manthorne, Jackie, 1946-

Ghost Motel

ISBN 0-921881-31-2

I. Title.

PS8576.A568G46 1994   C813'.54   C94-950179-4
PR9199.3.M36G46 1994

To Sylvia
May the dance never end.

Contents

"Where are those sunny skies she promised me?" complained Harriet Hubbley, uselessly castigating her absent lover. She squinted through the rain-spattered windshield, trying to keep her eyes on the nearly invisible centre line. Rain had started to fall just as she was crossing the rutted, decaying Champlain Bridge, and it had increased to a steady downpour during the half an hour she was delayed by repairs being completed on the bridge yet again this summer. Finally the traffic congestion had eased, and she left the island of Montreal and its sprawling suburbs behind and was soon crossing the border into the United States, passing through the wooded, mountainous scenery of Vermont and New Hampshire. She had planned on sightseeing, but her view was obscured by fog, and repeated rain squalls had forced her to keep her eyes on the road and to concentrate fully on her driving.

Harriet (better known as Harry to her close friends) grimaced as repeated forks of lightning lit the bilious sky and thunder rumbled loudly overhead. When the rain intensified, swirling in unpredictable currents which made it increasingly difficult to see, she wondered if it might be better to spend the night somewhere safe and comfortable rather than exhausting herself by driving straight through to Provincetown. It was nearly six o'clock, and she was just approaching the turn-off from Route 6 to Hyannis Port.

"Oh Judy, hang on for just one more night," Harry muttered unhappily as she reluctantly but sensibly decided to pack it in and find a place to stay. She had been driving since early morning: her eyes felt swollen and gritty, her stomach was empty, she had to go to the bathroom, and Bug, her small, dirt-beige, two-door hatchback, was nearly out of gas. She sighed, flicked the turn signal and took the exit to Hyannis Port.

Where to stop, she wondered, blinking at the flashing neon signs which shimmered unsteadily in the slanted rain. She drove for a couple of miles on the two-lane road, looking for a place to pull in, but most of the low-rise motels had posted neon "no vacancy" signs. Everybody wisely got off the road and went to bed early, she thought, slowing to a crawl as dense costal fog engulfed Bug.

There! Was that a vacancy sign up ahead? Yes it was! But it wasn't even lit — was the motel still open? It was worth finding out, Harry decided. She couldn't stand the thought of spending another mile behind the wheel, especially in weather like this. She concentrated on finding the entrance to the driveway, inched into the motel's parking lot, and parked Bug as close as possible to the dimly lit office. The paved courtyard between the two rows of deserted-looking motel units seemed unnaturally quiet, although she was reassured when she saw a few other cars.

"Good girl," she whispered affectionately, turning off the ignition, shutting the lights and patting Bug on the dash. Not every eight-year-old car was capable of being driven all day in stormy weather without a murmur of protest.

"I'll be right back," Harry said reassuringly, grinning at herself as she opened the door. Judy would laugh if she could hear her now, and she might be surprised, too, since during their ten years together, Harry hadn't confided that she quite regularly talked to inanimate objects when she was alone. Of course that was because she wasn't alone when she was with Judy…

Harry wondered whether her lover had slept the sleep of the faithful during the past five nights, or whether Judy's ex-lover Lorna had made an offer Judy couldn't refuse. Perhaps Judy had succumbed for old time's sake, seduced by the romantic allure of Provincetown and the underlying sensuality of so many lesbians in such a small town.

"Oh shut up," Harry grumbled to herself. "You weren't going to think about that any more." Warm rain enveloped her, soaking her to the skin before she was halfway from Bug to the office.

"Good evening," said the elderly woman behind the counter, giving Harry a welcoming smile.

"Hi," Harry replied, shaking herself like a wet puppy.

"Welcome to the West Yarmouth Seashore Motel. I'm Gertrude Cashin, better known as Gertie. I suppose you've been blown off course by this nasty storm," the woman remarked as she stood up. She was very thin and her skin was grey, almost pasty. She had short, mostly silver hair, and she was wearing an old-fashioned, flower-patterned dress.

"Yes," Harry replied, wiping rainwater from her brow with the back of her hand and then blinking several times to clear the excess moisture from her eyes.

"But you're positively soaked!" exclaimed Gertie. "I'll get you a towel."

"No, don't bother — I'm not cold," Harry politely reassured her.

"Nonsense," Gertie scoffed, walking toward the other side of the room. She moved slowly, holding herself erect with care, as if every step was painful. She looked sick, fatigued. Arthritis, perhaps, but Harry didn't ask.

"I've got a beach towel in my car ..." Harry said, her voice petering out as Gertie disappeared through an open doorway.

"Here, dry yourself," Gertie suggested, returning with a fluffy white towel.

Harry stopped protesting and used the towel to rub the excess moisture from her short, neatly cropped blond hair. She dried her arms and legs, and ineffectually patted her soggy tank top and cotton shorts.

"And then perhaps you wouldn't mind signing the registration book," Gertie requested, moving behind the counter again.

Harry wrapped the towel around her shoulders, leaned against the counter and printed her name, address and phone number on the thick, cream-coloured page, noting absently just before she sneezed several times in succession that the last person to sign it had been from Toronto.

"There now — you're catching cold," Gertie said with immediate sympathy. "I'm sure it's because of this miserable weather we've been having."

"No, really, it's just my allergies," Harry assured her, looking up from her casual perusal of the registration book. Everything in the office was covered with a thick layer of dust. She moved away from the counter, sneezing as she brushed dirt from the damp towel.

"Oh, don't mind that," Gertie said with a wave of dismissal. "My housekeeper has been sick a lot lately. There's some sort of vile stomach flu going around the Cape this summer, and she's come down with it twice."

"Oh," Harry managed to reply just before she sneezed again. Her sinuses ached.

"Bless you," Gertie said automatically. "So you'll want the room for one night, will you, Ms. — ?"

"Harriet Hubbley. Harry," Harry said with another sneeze. She fervently hoped that the Seashore Motel had clean rooms; otherwise, she would be sleeping in Bug tonight.

"Fine," Gertie said as she placed the cash Harry handed her in a drawer under the counter. "You're in number 24. It's on this side, at the far end of the row."

"Thanks," Harry said, taking the key from Gertie's hand.

"Would you like a cup of tea before you face that miserable storm again?" Gertie asked.

"I'd better find somewhere to have dinner and get settled in," Harry replied, stifling another sneeze. "But thanks, anyway."

"How about a coffee, then? With a little dash of brandy to get your blood circulating," Gertie suggested. "And I could certainly suggest a good restaurant, depending on what you like. We've no lack of superb restaurants on the Cape, as you probably know."

"Seafood," Harry replied immediately.

"Oh, you have to try the Sea Shanty, then," Gertie responded. "It's got the best lobster this side of Provincetown, and it's not expensive."

"Great," Harry said enthusiastically, her mouth filling with saliva at the thought of dining on moist, butter-dipped segments of steamed lobster.

"But have a coffee first," Gertie insisted. "It'll ward off the chill."

Harry was tempted. But she was starving, and brandy on an empty stomach, not to mention the devastating effect of that all-pervasive dust which already seemed to have coated her protesting lungs —

"There's no dust in there, either," Gertie said with a smile.

"Oh," Harry muttered, disconcerted.

"I do my own housekeeping in the back, you see," Gertie added. "So how about it? A little pick-me-up before dinner?"

"Well, why not?" Harry agreed, not wanting to be impolite in the face of the older woman's affable but dogged insistence. Perhaps she lived alone, didn't get much company, and relied on compliant guests for companionship.

"Good," Gertie replied cheerfully, leading the way from the office to a small — but dust-free, Harry was relieved to see — living room which was crammed with oversized, chintzy furniture from another era.

"So what do you do for a living, Harriet?" Gertie asked once Harry had settled into a large, upholstered chair which immediately enveloped her bone-weary body in soft, plush bliss.

"I teach," Harry said with an involuntary sigh.

"Well, you certainly don't sound very pleased about it," Gertie remarked.

"Oh, I don't mind," Harry said lightly, not wanting to become embroiled in a discussion of the merits or lack thereof of today's students, teachers and teaching methods or the perennially cash-starved education system.

"What subject do you teach?" Gertie asked.

"Physical education," Harry replied reluctantly, waiting for Gertie to laugh. Phys. ed. teachers were so stereotyped that she had grown to dislike mentioning what she did for a living.

"And do you teach little students or big ones?" Gertie inquired, making Harry smile.

"Big ones," Harry replied.

"Oh, no wonder you feel that way, then," Gertie said sympathetically.

"Actually, they're not so bad when they'll admit to being human," Harry told her. "Or that they actually like getting a little exercise sometimes." Ah, but the brandy was exquisite; it was taking the kink out of her stiff muscles and loosening the tight knot at the base of her skull.

"I admire your fortitude," Gertie replied as she rose stiffly from the twin of Harry's chair and filled her nearly empty mug with coffee. "Would you like more brandy?"

"No thanks," Harry said swiftly. "I still have some driving to do tonight."

"Oh, yes," Gertie said. "Dinner."

"I'm surprised you haven't got more customers, what with the storm and everything," Harry remarked as she watched Gertie refill her own mug and sit down again.

"To tell the truth, the Seashore Motel hasn't been in full operation for some time now," Gertie confided.

"You mean you don't have enough business?" Harry said, surprised. Cape Cod was bustling with tourists from spring until near-winter, and any half-decent motel from Buzzards Bay to Provincetown should have a waiting list.

"I'm retired, my dear," Gertie replied softly.

"Oh," Harry said, still nonplussed. Not that Gertie didn't look old, because she did. She didn't look to be in good health, either. Still, she could have sold the motel if she no longer wanted to run it at full capacity. Then again, perhaps she had enough money make ends meet without toiling 24 hours a day and half the night. After all, not everybody believed it was virtuous to work until you dropped from exhaustion.

"Yes, we all have to face it sooner or later," Gertie added philosophically, draining her mug.

"Have you ever thought of selling?" Harry asked swiftly, not particularly wanting to be lured into a conversation about aging, the degeneration of the body, death.

"Of course," Gertie replied promptly. "But all in good time. Although it won't be long now," she added thoughtfully.

"I see," Harry said, although she didn't.

"I had some business to finalize with the co-owner first," Gertie confided as she splashed more brandy into her mug.

"Oh," Harry responded, gently patting her growling stomach.

"Are you sure you wouldn't like another?" Gertie asked, waving the brandy snifter across Harry's line of vision.

"I'd better not — one more and I'll be three sheets to the wind," Harriet responded, placing her mug on the table beside her chair.

"How appropriately nautical," Gertie said with a hoarse laugh.

"I'm originally from Nova Scotia, although I've lived in Montreal for years," Harry explained.

"Well, my partner would certainly appreciate your choice of words," Gertie said.

"Oh yes?" Harry replied, her attention piqued by the use of the word "partner." Was Gertie referring to her business partner or to something more?

"She spent most of her life living on the coast, although not this one, unfortunately," Gertie said ruefully. "She settled in California."

"It must have been difficult for her to help you run the business from way out there," Harry said slowly, not knowing exactly how to respond.

"Quite difficult," Gertie agreed. "But then, the years passed swiftly, and a place this size wasn't so hard for one person to manage."

"I wondered why your sign wasn't turned on," Harry commented.

"There's no regular staff now, although I do keep a few rooms prepared," Gertie explained.

Harry yawned unexpectedly, her hand arriving at her mouth a split-second after it closed.

"For times like this," Gertie added.

"Uh-huh," Harry said politely.

"When a traveller like you needs a haven from the storm," Gertie said.

"Well, I'm certainly glad you were open tonight, or I'd likely be sleeping in my car," Harry reassured Gertie, wishing that there was someone there to reassure *her*. This woman was *strange*. "But I think it's time for some dinner."

They both rose from their chairs. Harry saw a spasm of pain appear on Gertie's face, but it disappeared briefly, leaving an exhausted look in her eyes. She knew it wouldn't be polite to ask; if Gertie wanted her to know what was wrong, she would tell her.

"It's the Sea Shanty, in case you've forgotten," Gertie reminded her.

"I haven't. Where exactly is it?" Harry asked, following Gertie from her living quarters into the dusty, ill-lit office.

"Turn right when you leave here. It's not far — about half a mile down the road, also on the right," Gertie replied.

"I'm sure I'll find it," Harry said. "And thanks for the coffee," she added. They shook hands, and Harry turned to leave.

"You're a lesbian too, aren't you, Harry?" Gertie said abruptly.

Harry was stopped in her tracks. "Er — yes."

"I thought so," Gertie said. "It's always nice to meet a fellow traveller in life. Well, enjoy your dinner."

Harry stared at her for a moment, smiled, nodded and left the office, gently closing the door behind her. How suitably seren-dipitous to meet another lesbian out here in the middle of nowhere, even if she was a little weird. And then she laughed at herself, because for a second she had actually imagined that Cape Cod was in the middle of nowhere. What a funny notion. Wait until she told Judy.

Bug started on the third try. Harry headed down the driveway and turned right. As long as she drove slowly, it shouldn't be hard to find the Sea Shanty, even with the premature darkness and reduced visibility. Still, she almost missed it, for in contrast to the garish, flashing neon signs of the other restaurants along the strip, the Sea Shanty's sign was hand-painted in old-fashioned script on a weather-beaten wood panel. She turned in at the last second and cautiously steered Bug across the cracked pavement of the deserted parking lot, her chest tightening when she realized that the low, rectangular building was in total darkness.

She rolled down the window and peered through the fog at the faded sign, verifying that it did indeed say "The Sea Shanty." Perhaps there was a second Sea Shanty nearby. Or perhaps Gertie had got the name wrong, or went out so seldom that she hadn't realized that the Sea Shanty was closed. Harry parked Bug close to the entrance, opened the door and slid from her seat, her eyes widening as she inspected the sagging roofline, peeling paint, weather-worn shingles, boarded-up windows and rotting staircase.

"Phew! This place sure didn't close last week," she muttered to herself, shivering in her wet shorts and tank top as the wind picked up and rattled a loose board. She scurried back into Bug's familiar surroundings and closed the door, taking one last look at the deserted building, wondering what Gertie had been thinking about when she had suggested this restaurant. Perhaps she had forgotten it was closed, or maybe she hadn't known. Or she could have been referring to another restaurant altogether. The word "sea" figured in the names of hundreds of costal restaurants from Newfoundland to Florida; more likely than not, Gertie had just got the names mixed up. Still, Harry thought as she sat in Bug's cosy warmth, watching the rising wind pick up a piece of cardboard and maul it, still, she needed something to eat. A cold breeze blew in through the partially-open window, splashing her with chilly rain and filling the car with a dank smell.

"Yuk! Let's get *out* of here," Harry said with some urgency, spooked by the strong smell of decay which seemed to have blown out of the car as swiftly as it had blown in, leaving her with a curled nose and the vision of uninhabited rooms with rotting wallpaper, sagging plaster, leaking pipes and caved-in ceilings, rooms where tiny but repulsive life forms did tiny and repulsive things she would rather not know about. She shivered and forced herself to stop exaggerating. The windows of the restaurant were securely boarded up, so the interior was probably watertight and vermin-free. Perhaps the Sea Shanty had been open as recently as last summer; wind-borne salt from the ocean, damp air and the bitter costal winter would swiftly age the untended exterior in no time.

"There's got to be some life in this town," she told Bug as she put the car in gear and headed for the road. "Let's go find it."

The Sea Shanty?" Harry's waiter said once he had seated her at a table and served her a glass of perfectly chilled chablis. "That was a pretty good restaurant. Did you eat there before it closed?"

"No. Somebody suggested I try it," she replied, staring at his skin-tight black trousers, long-sleeved white shirt and black bow tie. She felt underdressed, and hoped that her dishevelled hair and her inappropriate clothes, topped off with a moth-eaten cardigan which lived in the car for emergencies of this nature, didn't made her look like a bag lady.

"It's been closed for a couple of years now," he said, opening his order book and jotting something down. "Good food, but bad management. Does it every time."

"Really," Harry replied. The Sea Shanty wasn't that far from the Seashore Motel, so Gertie should have known. She must have passed the closed restaurant on her way to shop for groceries or to pick up something at the pharmacy or to accomplish any one of a multitude of things which necessitated leaving the house. "Oh, well," Harry muttered, opening her menu and ordering broiled lobster with rice pilaf and a tossed salad with Italian dressing on the side.

Harry broke off a piece of warm, crusty bread, spread a thick slab of butter on it and popped it into her mouth. Gertie had sent her on a wild goose chase. There must have been dozens of restaurants along this road, and yet she had recommended one which had been closed for at least two years. It didn't make sense.

She buttered another chunk of bread and chewed it with growing satisfaction, washing it down with a sip of wine. But Gertie had seemed fragile, as if every movement had given her pain. She had the thin, translucent skin of someone who was ill. Perhaps it was something chronic and growing worse with each passing day, she mused as the waiter served her salad. And Gertie lived alone. Her lover — and business partner, it seemed — was far away. What had she said, California? Whatever was ailing her, Gertie had to face it by herself. The thought of growing old and infirm alone had always disturbed Harry, so as she ate the last leaf of lettuce from her plate and waited for her lobster to be served, she resolved to visit the elderly woman as soon as she returned to the motel. Maybe there was something she could do, even if it was just to keep her company for a little while. Then her dinner arrived, and she set her mind to relishing fully every morsel of perfectly cooked lobster, accompanied by a second glass of wine.

Fuelled by her full stomach, energized by her natural curiosity and puzzled by Gertie's behaviour, Harry paid the rather hefty bill with one of her oft-abused credit cards and drove Bug back to the Seashore Motel. It was well after eleven and dark, the moon and stars hidden by the overcast sky. The rain had momentarily stopped, but the air was oppressively thick. Harry parked Bug by the office for the second time that evening and got out.

The light was on but the door was locked. Harry tried it a second time, just in case, but it really was locked. She searched the frame for a doorbell, but there wasn't one, so she knocked on the wood door with her bare knuckles. Time passed. She knocked again, then pressed her ear to the door, but all she could hear was the sound of traffic on the road. She had the feeling that there was no one there, but that was silly; where would Gertie go at this time of night?

Her fist paused on its way to the door, then opened and fell loosely to her side. She stood still, taking quick, shallow breaths, the unnatural silence nagging at her consciousness, then suddenly suffocating her.

"Hey," she growled, looking around. Something had startled her, but what? There was no one about, no one at all. Two other cars were parked in the courtyard, but all of the motel units were dark. The only illumination came from a bare spotlight on top of a chain link fence which encircled the far end of the courtyard, and it was swaying lazily in the breeze, casting more shadow than light.

"Hey," she repeated in a much more timid voice, moving swiftly toward Bug. "Let's get to our room."

The room was tiny, shabbily furnished with relics from the late '40s and early '50s, but clean. Harry locked and chained the door, grinning ironically at her useless precautions; anybody who was really determined to break in could simply put his foot through one of the flimsy panels. My, but she was spooked, and spooked good. It was too quiet. She felt like she was moving through a dead zone; everything in the Seashore Motel seemed to be isolated, static, petrified. But that was silly. Gertie was likely asleep. And maybe the owners of the other two cars had also turned in. After all, there probably wasn't much to do on a rainy evening on the Cape once you had finished dinner. Not at eleven o'clock, not unless you were prone to sitting in a bar and drinking yourself silly.

Her anxiety was not assuaged. She paced the room, listening expectantly for something, anything, for the sound of a door slamming or water running in the pipes in an adjacent unit or the electronic whine of a car ignition or the sound of voices raised in anger or passion or drunkenness. But there was nothing. Absolutely nothing. But that was because there wasn't anything, she assured herself. Everyone was tucked in for the night. This wasn't like the city, where people stayed up until all hours, where traffic never stopped, where buses and trucks rumbled down the street from dawn to dusk and back again.

She stripped and took a hot shower, washing the grit from her tired body. At this rate, she would probably lie awake all night listening to the silence, straining to hear a noise, any noise, until the thump of her heartbeat and the rasp of her breathing sounded so terrifyingly loud that she would be certain there was someone in the room with her.

But never mind, she thought as she towel-dried her hair. Tomorrow morning she would be in Provincetown, reunited with her lover. And she couldn't solve the world's problems, not even those of an sick old lady. She tucked herself into bed and sank into a deep sleep.

"A haven from the storm," Gertie was whispering, enunciating carefully, a peculiar leer disfiguring her handsome face.

"Yeah, something like that," Harry agreed politely, giving her a half-hearted smile. What the devil was she doing in Gertie's apartment? How had she got there? Never mind, you'd better drink up, she told herself, taking a large gulp of brandy. You've got a hell of a lot to finish before you can leave and go back to sleep, so you'd better be smart about it.

"Everyone needs a haven," Gertie said.

"Of course we do," Harry said, looking down at her brandy glass, dismayed to see that it was still full. She took another sip and realized that it wasn't brandy, it was dark rum. But she could have sworn … it had tasted exactly like brandy … she coughed, choking on the harsh, undiluted liquor.

But really, this was too silly. It wasn't even midnight, and she could barely keep her eyes open. The light from the lamp in the corner of Gertie's living room was flickering sporadically, growing dimmer and more distant with each erratic pulsation. The air itself seemed to be thickening around her, but that couldn't possibly be happening. Air was air, what did you add to thicken it? Flour? Cornstarch? She sipped her rum and giggled.

"Any storm," Gertie added. Why was she being so obscure, Harry wondered, half-drunk now. A haven was a safe place. Any fool knew that, even her students who were sixteen and hated to work up a sweat because it would either curl their hair or straighten it. Whatever. Except for the few jocks who made her teaching life worthwhile. For them, haven was a basketball court or a hockey rink or a soccer field and an opponent worth playing. But what about the storm? There had been a rainstorm today, hadn't there? No, that was too literal. A storm was a metaphor for what? Had something happened to Gertie? To Judy? Was something going to happen to her? Why couldn't she think straight? Because she was a lesbian? She giggled again and closed her eyes.

"We all get caught out in the storm at one time or another," Gertie whispered.

"I'm afraid I just can't stay awake," Harry apologized. "It must have been that long drive and the wonderful meal I had at the Sea Shanty." No, wait, that wasn't right. She hadn't been able to have dinner at the Sea Shanty but she couldn't remember why. Maybe she didn't have a reservation. Or they wouldn't let her in because she hadn't been dressed appropriately. Perhaps it had been closed for renovations. But it didn't matter. She lifted the brandy snifter to her lips and finished the rum, chug-a-lugging like a contestant in a beer-drinking contest.

"A storm blew into my life a long, long time ago," Gertie said dejectedly. "And it never blew out again."

But Harry wasn't listening. She burped, put her mug on the table and rose rather unsteadily from the easy chair. "Yes, and I certainly appreciate you telling me that," she said politely, shaking her head in an unsuccessful attempt to clear it. "But I finished my drink, so I can go now."

"Can you?"

Harry looked at the mug. She was certain she had finished the rum, but the mug didn't look empty. It seemed to be growing fuller as she stared at it. It must be a trick of the light, she thought, sitting down again.

"She went away and never came back again," Gertie whispered.

"Who?" Harry asked, picking up her mug. It was full. Gertie must have poured her another drink when she hadn't been looking.

"Who do you think?" Gertie replied impatiently.

Harry felt too embarrassed to admit that she was too inebriated to think.

"My lover," Gertie said with a sigh. "She ran all the way to California, and she never came back."

"You could have gone after her," Harry said. Would she get sick if she drank more rum? She carefully raised the mug to her lips and decided to find out.

"Not under the circumstances," Gertie replied, although she didn't offer an explanation.

"Well, you could have found another lover," Harry suggested, sipping rum from her mug. The inside of her mouth felt anaesthetized.

"People sometimes don't want another lover," Gertie snapped. "They want the one they had."

What did that have to do with her?

"You should know, Harriet."

Harry didn't.

Gertie grasped her wrist. She had a surprisingly strong grip for a frail old woman, but the fist around Harry's arm was cold, clammy.

"What's wrong?" Harry asked, squinting down a long, cyclonic tunnel at the unstable figure of the old woman.

Gertie's face pressed up against Harry's. How did that happen, Harry wondered, but before she had time to react she was shocked wide awake by the brilliance of Gertie's dark green eyes.

"Don't let her get away like I did," Gertie muttered, her face dissolving and reforming in a swift profusion of curves and wrinkles. It was just the light, Harry thought. Gertie should do something about that lamp, it was going to ruin her eyesight.

"Don't let who get away?" Harry asked, her own voice automatically aping Gertie's low, secretive tone.

"Your lover," Gertie murmured, her eyes sliding sideways.

"My lover?" Harry exclaimed, pulling her arm away, breaking the physical contact between them.

"Judy," Gertie said clearly.

"What do you mean?"

"You know very well what I mean," Gertie responded.

"Wait!" Harry shouted. "Tell me!"

Gertie laughed gently and turned away, growing smaller by the second. Where was she going? How could she be shrinking when she wasn't moving? How had she known Judy's name?

"It's way past your bedtime, child," Gertie said, her voice coming from far away.

"But you've got to tell me," Harry said urgently, teetering toward Gertie, her legs unsteady.

"A nice sleep, and you'll feel good as new," Gertie continued.

"Please," Harry begged, "I have to know." The old woman was disappearing. So much fog had seeped through the ill-fitting doors, the uncaulked windows, the irregular gaps in the clapboard, the tiny cracks between the floorboards, that Harry could barely see.

"Good night, sleep tight," came Gertie's sing-song voice.

"What do you mean?" Harry shouted impatiently, rubbing her tingling wrist.

"Pleasant dreams, sweet-heart-of-mine," Gertie warbled, and Harry heard an unseen door close with the heavy thud of finality.

"Ouch!" Harry exclaimed, her eyes snapping open. She had fallen out of bed. She sat on the floor and nursed her smarting elbow and her aching hip until the chill emanating from the damp carpet forced her to rise. Damn dream. She opened her dry mouth and closed it again. It meant nothing. There was no significance to a nightmare about an old woman she had met once. They were like ships passing in the night. Anyway, Gertie had probably been asleep when Harry had knocked on her door. She likely went to bed to sleep off all that brandy the minute Harry left for the Sea Shanty.

She didn't have to worry about Judy. After ten years, she certainly knew that Judy loved her; in fact, she had known it after ten days, but that wasn't the point. If Judy wanted to resurrect some erotic memories with one of her previous lovers, well, that was all right. Or so it should have been. Unfortunately, it wasn't.

She sighed, turned on the bedside lamp, and looked at her watch. It was two in the morning; if she left now, she would arrive in Provincetown before dawn. But she didn't want to know about Judy and Lorna's sleeping arrangements. Judy would tell her, but in her own good time. Judy would reveal the truth gradually, when she thought Harry was ready to accept it.

But it had been such a vivid dream.

Warning.

Premonition.

No. She had to stop exaggerating. It had just been a particularly bad dream. A first class nightmare she would forget when the sun came up and banished night.

She walked into the bathroom, splashed cold water on her face, and returned to the bedroom. She slipped into jeans and a sweatshirt, opened the door and stepped out into the fog, pocketing her key and closing the door quietly behind her. If she had any sense, she would be home in bed with her woman beside her, not trapped in this wet wasteland. She cursed the idiot who had invented tourism.

She walked through the fog, feeling like she was wading through wet wool. There was something wrong with this place. Stop it, she told herself. It was just a stupid, silly dream. She should go back to her room and get some sleep. Instead, she rapped forcefully on Gertie's door. There was no answer, but perhaps she hadn't expected one. She raised her hand to knock again and then hesitated; she wanted an explanation, but was she ready for another conversation with a eccentric old woman who had already managed to scramble her senses and disturb her equilibrium, even if it had only been in a dream? It was two o'clock in the morning; Gertie would think she was demented, especially if she said, "I dreamed you said some stuff about storms and havens and warned me about Judy and then disappeared in a wisp of smoke." That would never do.

Her resolve broke, and with it her nervousness. She went back to her room, slid into bed and immediately fell into an exhausted, dreamless sleep.

3

Sunlight was essentially cheerful and the lack of same could drive even a perfectly normal dyke to dreary, irrational thoughts about bumps in the night, not to mention unfaithful lovers. And Bug didn't particularly want to face the day either, Harry discovered as she gently caressed the clutch and the gas pedal with her toes and stroked the steering wheel with her fingertips while murmuring decreasingly endearing terms, impatient to put this dreadful place and its desolate air of desertion far behind her. The vividness of her dream had shocked her, as had the strangeness of it. In contrast to her strong desire to speak with Gertrude Cashin the night before, Harry had wanted nothing more than to leave, so she had dropped her key through the mail slot in the door rather than knocking on it to see if Gertie was awake. It was early, she had rationalized, so why disturb her?

"Can I help?" came a disembodied male voice through the rain-streaked window.

Harry stopped trying to start the car and lowered the window an inch.

"Maybe I could be of some help?" he suggested again with dour uncertainty.

"Maybe," Harry reluctantly agreed. He was thin, bald, effete, and about as middle-aged as she was. She could take him in a couple of seconds if she had to. On that basis, she opened the door and stepped into a puddle which immediately soaked her running shoe.

"Clifford Jones, from Toronto," he announced promptly, his pale hand streaking up from beside his thigh.

"Harriet Hubbley, from Montreal," she replied, firmly shaking his damp fingers. "And this is Bug."

"I'm in sales," he added as they rounded Bug and Harry lifted the hood.

She squinted at him through fine droplets of rain before they inspected Bug's intestines, trying not to let the tackiness of it all depress her further. A nearly deserted motel, a boarded-up restaurant, a sick old woman who treated her to a nightmare and then, for good measure, facilitated her introduction to a travelling salesman named Clifford. She wondered whether Gertie had something in mind for an encore. Listen here, Bug, she silently but firmly exhorted the drooping fan belt of her sulking car, get over this indigestion of yours so we can get out of this place.

"Doesn't like the rain, I'll bet," commented Clifford.

"Right," Harry grimaced, rubbing her knuckles across the radiator. What did Bug want? Had she gone on strike for thicker oil? A taste of American gas? A lube job? To get in out of the rain? Or did she miss Judy? She could at least give Harry a hint, but no, she just sat there sagging on all fours, quiet as a mouse while a man who obviously knew as much about the innards of cars as he did about the innards of mice hummed and hawed, which annoyed the hell out of Harry.

"Maybe she just flooded," Clifford suggested.

"Sure," Harry replied sourly, opening the door and sliding into the driver's seat. One man, one instant expert. Now you start, she scolded the silent car as she pushed the clutch into the floor with one foot and gassed her with the other, hearing Bug rumble and then shake with lazy protest.

"There you go!" exclaimed Clifford. "She was probably just a little too wet."

"See you around," Harry said with an obvious lack of conviction.

"Not if I see you first," Clifford said with a grin.

She decided to leave before he suggested breakfast. She gave him a perfunctory wave which bore more than a passing resemblance to a karate chop, put Bug in gear and sped from the parking lot, escaping from West Yarmouth and the nearly deserted Seashore Motel, the rotting Sea Shanty Restaurant, the mysterious Gertie and the congenial Clifford Jones, travelling salesman. She slowly navigated the narrow, two-lane blacktop and took the first right to Route 6 East.

How many miles to Provincetown, she wondered as Bug's balding tires revolved on the slick highway, dispatching rivulets of rainwater to the deep gutters. How many hours to Provincetown and Judy?

Shortly after she left West Yarmouth, the rain stopped and she started making good time. When her stomach was so empty that it was nearly touching her spine, she pulled into Wellfleet and had a superb meal of lobster and home fries in a shack by the water. The lobster was served with the shell cut, so all she had to do was fork out the tender, moist meat and dip it in melted butter. Quenching her thirst with a mug of local ale, she leaned her elbows on the table and stared out the window.

The rain clouds were scudding swiftly out to sea, and high overhead, wispy clouds were replacing them. It was going to be a fine day after all. The sun would probably be shining before she reached Provincetown. Harry finished her ale and glanced at her watch; it was time to face the proverbial music, to see if her lover was still hers. She drove to the outskirts of Wellfleet and stopped at a gas station to feed Bug, who responded by humming along silently. She thrust her foot down on the gas pedal, pushing Bug to the speed limit and then over it, and before long she was on the outskirts of Provincetown. Following Judy's directions, she turned onto a residential street which led to the older section of the city. She parked Bug in front of Lorna's house and got out of the car, breathing deeply in appreciation of the fragrant maritime air. She walked up the weedy cement walk to the porch, and knocked on the door.

At first she thought no one was home, and was about to turn away when the inside door opened.

"Yeah?" said a slight, scantily clad woman.

"Is Judy here?" Harry asked.

"No," the woman replied.

"What?" Harry asked in surprise.

"She's not here," the blond repeated. Her long, blond hair was pulled back in a messy pony tail, and she was dressed in tight short-shorts and a torn, stained tank top which had been carelessly hacked off just below her breasts.

"Where is she?" What a dump this place was. Paint was flaking off the screen door, and the screen itself was ripped in several places. The roof was sagging and very likely leaked, the wood around the windows was pock-marked, and the exterior of the house was in urgent need of paint.

"She's in North Truro with Lorna," the blond woman answered in a bored tone, fiddling with the band of faded pink elastic holding her pony tail in place.

"What are they doing there?" Harry asked, thinking ruefully that she had just passed the North Truro motel strip on her way into Provincetown.

"Looking for a place for Judy to stay, I guess," the blond answered.

"But I thought we were staying here," Harry responded, feeling puzzled.

"Oh, you mean you're Judy's girlfriend?" the blond asked, leaning closer to the rusty screen to get a better look at Harry.

"Yes, that's right. I'm Harriet Hubbley," Harry replied, wishing she would open the door and invite her in out of the heat. Maybe the house was a mess.

"Great," the blond said with a noticeable lack of enthusiasm. "I'm Mickey. Sorry I can't ask you in, but I'm right in the middle of my meditation class."

"Oh," Harry responded, nonplussed. She was taken aback at Mickey's blatant lack of hospitality; after all, the house obviously had more than one room, and she was capable of sitting unobtrusively in a corner and waiting for Judy and Lorna to return from North Truro while Mickey meditated. At least the woman could show her to a back garden where she could relax after her long drive.

"See ya around," Mickey said with a ghost of a smile as she began to turn away.

"But when will they be back?" Harry asked swiftly, before Mickey had time to close the inside door.

"I dunno," Mickey replied with a disinterested shrug. "Lorna's got to work tonight, though," she added as an afterthought just before the door swung all the way shut.

"Thank for nothing," Harry muttered to the unpainted door. She gave an amused snort, walked back to Bug, opened the door and got in. It was starting to cloud over again, but it was still too hot to sit in Bug for more than a couple of minutes. Deciding to lock the car and explore on foot, she rummaged through the cluttered glove compartment until she found the street map of Provincetown she had picked up at the gas station in Wellfleet. Provincetown was supposed to be a lesbian haven — damn, there was that word again, she thought, remembering Gertie's strident warning. She suddenly felt as troubled as she had the night before, when the hulk of the deserted Sea Shanty Restaurant had cruelly mocked her and the close, silent atmosphere of the Seashore Motel had immersed her in floating, nameless anxiety. The map fell through Harry's fingers and slipped to the floor.

She sighed, wiped the sweat from her brow and bent down to retrieve it. This was ridiculous. She knew as well as the next person that dreams weren't real. Gertie had been strange, but so were millions of other people. It had only been a nightmare, vivid, disturbing and fantastic to be sure, but still nothing more than a bothersome dream. In the full light of day she felt chagrined about how afraid she had been.

"Hi, there!"

She jumped with surprise and the map flew from her hand a second time, its folds unfurling and slapping against the dashboard.

"Oh! You startled me!" Harry exclaimed. Judy was leaning down and looking at her through the open car window, and Harry smiled up at her familiar face. How she loved those high cheekbones, that long, thick, dark hair, those intense, intelligent brown eyes!

"I thought you'd fallen asleep, or that you were suffering from heat prostration," her lover commented. "Give me a kiss, why don't you?"

"What, right here on the street?" Harry said, scandalized.

"Right here, over there, anywhere," Judy replied exuberantly. "It's Provincetown, silly! Everybody, but everybody is gay!"

Harry noticed for the first time how many same-sex couples there were. Several of them were holding hands or had rather casually draped their arms around their partners' shoulders or waists.

"So where's my kiss?" Judy said in a more serious tone. Harry grinned and drew her lover down for a long, lingering kiss. Five days was five days, after all, and even after ten years, that was far too long for Harry to be without her woman. And without sex. Whether Judy had also gone without for five days was another question, one which Harry did not want to ask at this particular moment, although it was certainly on her mind.

"Am I ever glad you're here," Judy said as they broke apart.

"Me too," Harry responded nervously, wondering if Judy was planning to confess. She hoped not; she didn't think she could deal with it so soon. Actually, she would rather never deal with it, but that was something which was outside of her control.

"Come out of that car before you faint from the heat," Judy said, her tone light again. She pulled the door open and reached in for Harry.

"It is sort of hot," Harry agreed as she grasped Judy's hand and got out of Bug. "Let me lock up."

"That's a good idea. We can walk over to Commercial and have something to eat," Judy replied.

"Sounds great," Harry said, winding up Bug's window and locking the door.

"Just wait til you see Commercial. It's the main street. More importantly, that's where all the dykes are," Judy said enthusiastically.

"Sounds even better," Harry said with a smile.

"I'll just get my suitcase and put it in the trunk," Judy said, turning toward Lorna's ill-kempt house.

"What's going on, hon?" Harry asked softly, reaching out and touching her lover's arm. "I thought we were supposed to stay here."

"Can we talk about that later?" Judy asked, not meeting Harry's gaze.

"Sure," Harry said reluctantly.

Judy looked so grateful that Harry experienced a vague sense of discomfort. "Want me to come along?" she asked, gesturing at the house.

"I think I can carry my suitcase by myself," Judy responded with a grin.

"You know what I mean," Harry scolded.

"Yes I do, but really, I can manage," Judy replied. "Thanks anyway."

"Sure," Harry said. She leaned against Bug and watched Judy disappear behind the wobbly screen door, resigned to never having the privilege of getting one single, solitary look at the interior of Lorna's house, or at Lorna herself, for that matter.

Five long minutes passed. Harry stifled the urge to barge into the house in pursuit of her lover. Her impatience corralled, she then attempted to stop her imagination from fantasizing all-too-vivid images of protracted and probably passionate embraces as Judy and Lorna bid each other a fond farewell. She told herself that Judy wouldn't do that while she was waiting outside. Then she told herself that Judy probably hadn't finished packing before she and Lorna drove to North Truro. When she was desperate enough to fervently pray that Judy had interrupted the apparently sacrosanct meditation class and was saying good-bye to the decidedly anti-social Mickey, Harry conceded defeat and started up the path to the house.

The screen door flew open and Judy and a woman Harry assumed was Lorna rushed out. Neither of them saw Harry beat a hasty retreat, scurrying backwards to lean casually against Bug with the picturesque street as backdrop. They were too busy concentrating on each other. They were talking in vehement but low voices, Judy's eyebrows drawn in an intense, angry knot Harry had rarely witnessed, Lorna's expression impatient and somewhat ruthless.

They stopped halfway down the walk. Harry couldn't hear what either of them was saying, but she felt threatened on Judy's behalf because Lorna was very obviously reading her the riot act, and threatened on her own behalf when she saw Judy's eyes glisten with tears. Suddenly Judy turned and walked swiftly away from Lorna, her suitcase banging against her bare leg.

"I'll take it," Harry offered.

"Open the door," Judy replied in a harsh voice.

"But I thought you wanted to walk —"

"We'll park somewhere else," Judy interrupted, holding out her hand. "Now give me the key."

Harry surrendered it and watched Judy open the door and push her suitcase into the back seat. Judy slid into the driver's seat, reached across, and unlocked the door on the passenger side.

"Come on," she urged as Harry stood on the sidewalk staring down at her.

Harry nodded and walked around Bug, glancing at Lorna, who was watching them silently, her face impassive but pale.

"Come on," Judy repeated impatiently as Harry got into the passenger seat and fumbled with her seat belt.

"It's okay," Harry mumbled, feeling totally out of her depth. She grabbed the dash to steady herself as Judy made a U-turn, Bug's tires complaining at the unfamiliar exertion, the clutch jamming for a second when Judy pounced on it too soon.

"Judy," Harry complained as her lover gassed Bug, who responded like a dog off the leash and rounded the corner on two squealing tires.

"You're right. I'm going too fast," Judy replied, her stern face breaking into an apologetic smile. She glanced at Harry and then turned her attention back to the crowded street, but she didn't slow down.

Harry was certain that Judy was going to get them killed. She tried to settle her nervous stomach as it reacted to Bug's sudden starts and stops, bracing herself one final time as Judy braked abruptly and backed into a tight parking spot, getting it right the first time. Disgusting, Harry thought; Judy could have a fight with her ex-lover, be stuck with her current lover on her hands when she would probably like to be alone to lick her wounds, and yet she could still park on a dime.

"What's going on?" Harry asked.

Judy withdrew the key from the ignition and Bug sputtered and died. "Later, okay? I haven't had anything to eat today and I'm starving." She opened the door and got out. "Commercial is just down there." She set out at a determined clip, leaving Harry with no choice but to follow.

"Wait for me!" she cried, and Judy paused until she reached her side and then started off again, forcing Harry to struggle to keep up with the swift pace she was setting. She followed Judy around the corner to Commercial Street, where they nearly collided with a group of laughing women.

"Wow!" Harry exclaimed, her attention shifting from Judy's anger to the sight in front of her. "This is a lesbian paradise!"

"What did I tell you?" Judy said, her hands on her hips, a tentative smile gracing her lips.

"Words fail me," Harry admitted.

"That must be a first," Judy teased.

Harry didn't answer. She glanced from one woman to another, noting that other woman were doing the same; making eye contact, evaluating the possibilities, sometimes pausing to smile, to take a chance and actually speak, sometimes responding to unspoken signs and signals and moving on. Street cruising. Harry tried to imagine lesbians always being as free and open as this, but she couldn't. That made her feel sad. She watched two middle-aged women join hands and leave the sidewalk, picking their way between cars trapped in a long line which was moving about as fast as your average unhurried turtle. She stared at two women who were leaning against the window of a boutique, kissing each other as if they were the only people in the world.

"Come on, Harry, I'm going to starve if I don't eat something," Judy said.

Harry felt Judy take her hand and lead her along the sidewalk. They passed two women arguing, a woman selling tee-shirts covered with lesbian slogans, another woman handing out flyers about the regular Sunday tea dance at one of the bars, a couple of guys holding hands while eating ice cream.

"Are you in the mood for seafood?" Judy asked.

"Always," Harry confirmed. "You know me."

"Then let's go in here. It's one of the best places in town," Judy told her.

"Okay," Harry answered, taking one last, bemused look at the action on the street.

"You'll get over it," Judy said with a laugh as she pushed through the swinging doors.

"What?"

"You'll get used to seeing so many dykes," Judy explained.

"I certainly hope not," Harry fervently replied.

Judy laughed again.

Patience was definitely not Harry's middle name, but she tried. She munched on crusty French bread, had two servings of salad liberally covered with tangy house dressing, carefully removed every morsel of perfectly steamed lobster from its shell, and kept her questions to herself. They talked about Montreal. Judy wanted to know all the latest gossip, and Harry complied. It was summer, and their friends were taking full advantage of the short, hot season to become embroiled in torrid love affairs or to cheat their lovers for no good reason or to spend all their time complaining about said scandalous behaviour while being secretly jealous that some dykes they knew were leading exciting although perhaps not envious lives.

When coffee arrived — two very rich, hot cappuccinos — Harry was certain that Judy would explain, but no. An uncomfortable silence ensued. Harry had exhausted her store of news over dinner; they had only been separated for five days, and even the most reckless of their friends wasn't capable of irrevocably complicating her life in such a short period of time. Discomfort crept in with the cool, early evening sea breeze, and Harry's heart grew as chilly as her fingers and toes. She and Judy were never at a loss for words with each other, *never.*

"Let's go, hon," Judy said.

Harry nodded. "Is the motel far?"

"No. Just outside of town," Judy replied.

They picked their way through the strollers on Commercial Street. It was dusk, and the sky was crimson with the promise of another hot, sunny day.

"Want me to drive?"

"No, I will. I know the way," Judy said, opening the passenger door for Harry.

The Cliff Top Motel was just that; a rambling, one-storey motel built at the top of a steep, rocky cliff. Their room overlooked the ocean, and from the window Harry could see a wood staircase leading down to the beach, where whitecaps were roughly slapping the white sand.

"It's beautiful," she said, turning to Judy, who was unpacking her suitcase into the top drawer of the dresser.

"Yes," Judy replied, but she didn't look up.

"You should come see," Harry suggested.

"Later."

Harry gave up and sat down on the bed. Everything was slightly askew, and it made her feel timid. "Want to walk down to the beach?"

"Later," Judy said again, zipping up her suitcase.

"But it'll be dark soon," Harry said.

Judy pushed her suitcase into a corner of the closet and looked at Harry. "Okay. Let's go for a walk, then."

They were the only people on the beach. The roar of the waves, the primordial smell of the sea and the taste of salt on her lips invigorated Harry. She didn't consciously miss the ocean when she was away from it, but each time she returned to the sea, she realized that its influence would never entirely leave her. As a child, she often sat quietly on a patch of moss in the woods or on a large stone on the beach and watched the waves, their steady motion producing in her a feeling of total peace, of oneness with the universe.

"Isn't this great?" she shouted at Judy. She picked up a flat stone and side-armed it into the water, watching it skip three times before sinking, and then dropped to her knees to look for shells, pocketing several tiny periwinkles.

"I slept with Lorna."

The perfection of sand, sea and sky shattered. Harry's latest discovery, an unbroken crab shell, fell unnoticed from her hand. She stood up and slowly brushed wet sand from her knees. The incoming tide pushed a wave high on the beach, and cold water broke over her feet, soaking her sandals and splashing her legs, but she didn't notice.

"I said —"

"I heard you," Harry sighed.

"You're shivering. And wet. Let's go up."

Harry felt devastated. And bitter. Through ten years of monogamy, she had purposefully brushed off all approaches from other women, including some she was incredibly attracted to, physically or otherwise. She had also refused to become involved in flirtations with no serious intent but much temporary danger, or to sleep with her friends, and for what? To be betrayed like this? She tried to imagine Judy in bed with Lorna, but failed. Perhaps it was just as well.

"It wasn't planned," Judy said. "It just happened."

That's what they all say, Harry thought, jealousy curdling into meanness. A hot summer's night in Provincetown, a little too much wine, the lure of an old lover. She could see it all. It was so predictable, and so tawdry in its predictability that she felt disappointed in Judy.

"Let's go up," Judy urged.

It was growing dark; the sky was purple with night. They stumbled up the stairs, and by the time they reached their room, Harry was shivering, her teeth chattering from the chilly night air, from her wet jeans and sandals, from the indigestible truth.

"Why don't you take a shower? That will warm you up," Judy suggested, retreating into practicality. She raised the thermostat and the box heater beneath the window rumbled into life.

Harry stripped in the bathroom with the door closed, hiding her invisible wounds. She looked down, unable to identify with her full drooping breasts, her curved, fat-padded belly with its blond bush just below or her narrow hips and sturdy thighs. Perhaps it was an impossibility born of despair, or hatched in a moment of disillusionment, but at that moment, she felt disembodied.

She stepped into the shower and gasped as hot water streamed over her chilled flesh. The pressure was high, and needles of water sluiced the sea salt from her body and made her skin tingle. She shampooed her hair until it was squeaky clean and washed it again. She scrubbed her skin until it turned red in protest, and then gave up; there were things to be said, and she could not escape saying them.

"Here."

Harry saw the open brandy bottle on the bedside table and took the glass from Judy's hand. "I lied when I said I trusted you and now I feel like I'm paying for not telling the truth. I thought I was just being silly, that my insecurity was making me act like an idiot. Somehow, though, I knew what was going to happen. But thinking that something might take place and knowing for certain that it did are two different things," she said, wrapping the towel tightly around her and sitting on the edge of the bed.

"I know. I'm sorry."

Harry sipped the brandy without really tasting it. "We never actually promised that we wouldn't, but there must have been a damn good reason why we didn't, not once in ten whole years."

"I'm sorry," Judy whispered.

Sorry. Sorry, sorry, sorry. Of course she was sorry. No matter how many times she said it, it would still mean nothing. Or everything. Or worse yet, anything: I'm sorry I didn't listen. I'm sorry, but I just didn't think. I'm sorry I didn't love you enough. Or that I loved you too much.

"I never wanted to hurt you."

Harry sighed, because she knew it was true. She finished the brandy and tried not to think of her nightmare.

"Let's go to bed," Judy suggested, turning her back to undress. Harry looked and then averted her eyes, knowing it was illogical but still afraid that she would see Lorna's fingerprints on Judy's skin. She unwrapped the wet towel from her body, draped it over a chair, slid between the sheets and pulled them up to her neck.

July switched off the light and joined her in bed. "Let me make love to you," she whispered, her hands resting lightly on Harry's breasts.

"No," Harry replied emphatically, turning on her side.

She felt Judy's breath on her neck, her breasts pressing into her back. Judy gently kissed her shoulder, and ran her hand over Harry's breast. When one nipple grew hard, Judy reached lower and brought the other to the same state.

Harry stirred, aroused. Passivity did not suit her, but confusion forestalled her active participation. She wanted to turn, to take Judy in her arms and obliterate Lorna's presence, to replace Lorna's fingerprints with her own and re-establish possession, ownership. But that impulse was wrong. She didn't own Judy, and she never would. The jealousy she felt was a reflection of her own insecurities. Rationally, she knew that Judy hadn't betrayed her by making love with Lorna; if she had betrayed anyone, it had been herself, although that was for Judy to conclude, not Harry. They had not relinquished their separate identities when they had become a couple. What they owed each other was honesty and respect, not some lesbian variation on selflessness, or love on demand.

Judy's hand slid down over Harry's belly and parted her thighs.

"This is different," Harry said gruffly.

"It certainly is," Judy replied breathlessly.

Harry started to turn around.

"No, stay like that," Judy whispered. "I like it." Her fingers explored, stroked, teased.

"But I want to —"

"Later," Judy said.

Harry surrendered and concentrated on herself, taking comfort from Judy's familiar scent, her murmured endearments, her knowing hands, her loving touch. She could hear the rhythmic heartbeat of the ocean, she could see in her mind's eye how the water was caressing the waiting shore. The waves rose high over her, bubbling until their frothy tendrils were spent, enveloped by the porous sand in continuous renewal.

And then she turned over and took matters into her own hands.

This is such a paradise," Judy sighed. "I could stay here forever. The whole summer, anyway."

Harry looked at her and smiled.

They were sitting at a wrought-iron table on the patio of a small café just off Commercial, the spectacular harbour off to one side and the town on the other. It really was quite idyllic. Harry sipped her coffee and bit into a croissant. She wasn't hungry, but she couldn't resist; the croissant was buttery and marbled with chocolate.

She and Judy had made love well into the night, but being reassured was one thing and regaining her equilibrium quite another. It was going to take time. She took another bite, washed it down with coffee, and yawned. She had slept badly, restlessly, waking with a dry mouth and red-rimmed eyes. She had dreamed of Gertrude Cashin, of an inexplicable urgency, of despair. Whose, she didn't know. The meaning of her dream was elusive; most of the details had remained behind, and she wasn't interested in recovering them. No, let them stay where they were.

"I want to tell you what happened," Judy said suddenly.

Harry dropped her croissant on her plate and looked across the table at her lover. "I'm not sure I want to know," she admitted. "But if you have to …"

"I don't *have* to, but I'd *like* to," Judy responded.

Harry wasn't ready. But if she said that to Judy, she might never mention it again. They had always shared their fears and anxieties as well as their hopes and dreams, and she didn't want that to stop. If she discouraged Judy from talking about something as important as this, they might never be as close again. So she nodded and said, "tell me."

"Lorna is perhaps the most intelligent, strong-willed woman I've ever met. And while these are admirable characteristics in a person, they can be very alienating when carried to extremes. That's why we broke up."

"I know."

"She thought she was smarter than me, which was true, but you can't build a successful relationship on that premise. Having a lot of willpower is great, but it's incredibly damaging when it turns to rigidity. You can't talk to a person who doesn't respect your point of view or even admit that you have the right to have one. And in the end, you can't go on living with them, either," Judy said.

Harry nodded.

"I wasn't sure what to expect when she invited us to stay with her. That's why I wanted to come down by myself. I didn't want to put you in the position of having to be polite just because she was an old lover of mine, or of having to suffer through a week of her viciousness. But when I got here, she was all peaches-and-cream," Judy continued. "She wanted to know all about what I'd been doing, my job, you. We got along famously. Then we decided to spend an evening out on the town, just the two of us, and you know how darn romantic Provincetown can be —"

"This is my first time here," Harry responded.

"So don't make it easy for me."

"I can't," Harry admitted.

"I suppose not. Anyway, Lorna can turn on the charm when she wants to."

Harry sipped her coffee and waited.

Judy dropped her cup into its saucer so carelessly that the resulting clatter turned the heads of women at neighbouring tables. "Oh, hell! Why am I trying to make excuses for myself? It was seductive and I let myself be seduced."

Harry lifted her cup but it was empty. Caffeine overdose be damned, she thought, gesturing to the waitress. Maybe they had decaf.

"I convinced myself that because Lorna was an old lover, it would be safe to be charmed by the town, by the night," Judy said after the waitress had refilled their cups.

"And by the woman," Harry said bitterly.

"I'm sorry," Judy whispered.

Harry nodded and bit her lip. She wasn't being fair. "Go on."

"Maybe I shouldn't," Judy said. "This is too much for you right now, isn't it?"

"I said to go on, and I meant it," Harry said through clenched teeth.

"Are you sure?"

Harry didn't reply because she was afraid she would scream or worse, say something nasty. This was much harder than she had imagined, which in a perverse way, was a good thing; if she had known how awful she was going to feel, she might have turned Bug around and high-tailed it back to Montreal.

"I had forgotten how good it could feel to be with Lorna when things were going well," Judy said. "We wandered up and down Commercial, found a great place for dinner, had a few drinks, watched the sunset. I let my guard down because it felt so familiar. All of it came back, including our attraction to each other."

Harry drank coffee to console herself. It didn't work.

"It was just a comfortable buzz in the beginning. Something which makes everything seem better than it really is, which makes you feel glad to be alive. The food is perfect, the wine is exemplary, jokes are funnier, the woman more intelligent, wittier, devastatingly seductive. And you feel like the most attractive woman in the world. You know what I mean," Judy continued, looking at Harry for confirmation.

"Yeah," Harry said, grudgingly.

"In the end I got caught up in it, and when we went back to her house, we made love," Judy said.

Harry fiddled with her spoon.

"Don't you want to know?" Judy asked.

"What good will it do?"

"It might stop all your fantasizing, for one thing," Judy replied wryly.

She knows me all too well, Harry thought ruefully. "Don't make it into a joke!" she retorted.

"Sorry. I didn't mean it that way," Judy answered. "And for your information, the sex was fine. Just fine. *That* was never a problem in our relationship. Look, Lorna and I had a couple of good years together. I cared deeply for her. There are some things you never forget — including the women you love. I sometimes wonder if our bodies become imprinted with each other's in some instinctive, primordial way. Perhaps that's too far out. But you have to admit that memories of loved ones literally last a lifetime, and they're not only emotional, they have a physical component as well. In any case, Lorna is part of my history. Living with her was a mistake which I regretted then, and I still regret it now. I should have known better than to be fooled by her flirtatious banter, because she hasn't changed. It was just more of the same."

Harry realized that the croissant she had so eagerly devoured was stuck in her throat.

"We only made love once, Harry. When I woke up the next morning and listened to Lorna pontificate about the miserable state of her relationship with that poor girl Mickey sitting right at the breakfast table with us, I knew I wanted nothing more to do with her. Not that Mickey seemed to care — she just sat there and ate her granola as if Lorna was talking about the weather rather than how unhappy she was living with her, how deplorable their sex life was and how witless Mickey was."

"She sounds like a real charmer," Harry commented.

"Lorna never was the most sensitive person in the world," Judy replied. "But I also realized how truly wrong it had been of me to do that to you. We hadn't discussed the possibility of either of us becoming involved with other women, and it was unfair of me to act before we had come to an understanding about it," Judy said. "As it is, I've forced the issue, and I wholeheartedly regret it."

Harry cleared her throat, but the croissant was still there. Or maybe it was her whole stomach. "Have you been thinking of having an affair?"

"Not precisely," Judy replied. "But I wonder whether we're both limiting ourselves by not letting our relationships with other women develop naturally," Judy replied. "But I've been so stupid. I wanted to bring this up without threatening you, and look what I've done instead."

"By developing naturally, I assume you mean sexually," Harry said, attempting to maintain a neutral tone of voice as the foundations on which she thought their relationship was built came tumbling down.

"Not necessarily," Judy answered. "But if it did happen, would it necessarily be wrong? Look, Harry, I feel infinitely more guilty about having done this without discussing it with you first than I do about the sex itself."

Harry knew that some couples had open relationships. She also realized on a purely theoretical level that there were more intimate things in life than sex. The love between close friends, for instance. Having sex could actually be less intimate than a long talk with a good friend. The sex shouldn't matter. Shouldn't, but did. "When I think of you with somebody else, I get so jealous that it hurts," Harry confessed. If Judy laughed at her, she was going to get up and leave.

"You always did have butch tendencies," Judy said affectionately. "But jealousy is such a destructive emotion. Useless, too."

"Maybe I'm not giving you enough. Maybe you're bored with the same old thing after all these years," Harry blurted.

"That's not true, Harry, and you know it. I want to spend the rest of my life with you, but I won't deny I've thought about making love with other women. Why should one preclude the other? Haven't you ever thought about it?"

Harry shook her head. There had been moments when temptation was strong, but she had always resisted. She had never permitted anything to develop, not even in her mind.

"I know that you feel hurt, and I'm sorry. But nothing has changed. I still love you; I'll *always* love you," Judy whispered. "And we don't have to discuss these ideas of mine. Not now."

"Not yet, you mean," Harry said, feeling miserable.

"Never, if that's the way it has to be," Judy responded.

Oh, that was just fine and dandy. If it never came up again, it would be her fault, and she would spend the rest of her life with the sword of Damocles hanging over her.

"What can I do to make you feel better?"

"Nothing," Harry answered honestly.

Judy sighed. "I'm sorry. Oh lord, I sound like a broken record, don't I?" she added ruefully.

"Look, let's just stop talking about it, okay?" Harry suggested, wishing it would be so easy to erase it from her mind.

Judy nodded and they sat in silence until the waitress offered them a refill. Judy accepted, Harry didn't. She didn't want anything except the return of her peace of mind.

"So what do you want to do today?" Judy asked.

"I don't know."

"Do you want me to get a newspaper and see what's going on?"

"Sure."

Harry watched her lover cross the street and enter a store, and then lost sight of her in the crowd. Judy had been thinking about things which she hadn't shared. Important things, like the nature of their relationship. Harry was devastated. A fleeting sense of rebellion rushed through her, leaving her shaken. But retaliation would do no good, and besides, she didn't want anybody but Judy.

"Here," Judy said, tossing the first section of the newspaper in Harry's lap. "I'll check the second section."

"Right," Harry replied, trying to sound interested.

"Do you want to go to a movie, or spend the afternoon in a bar playing pool, or go back to the motel and go swimming?"

"Let's see what's happening in town, okay?" Harry answered.

"Sure," Judy said, glancing at Harry for reassurance but not finding it. She dropped her gaze to the paper.

Harry stifled a sigh and leafed through the newspaper. There were movies, but none she wanted to see. One of the theatres had scheduled a matinee performance, but they were doing a play about AIDS, and there was too much of that in real life to spend part of her vacation being alternately angered and saddened and left with a lingering angst about the inescapable reality of dead friends and lost companions. So much waste ...

"Let's go back for a swim," she said, folding the newspaper and dropping it into her tote-bag.

"Wouldn't you rather spend the afternoon sitting in a bar by the ocean?" Judy replied.

Harry shrugged.

"Sipping a tall, cool drink and watching the boats, the seagulls, the women?" she ventured a smile, and Harry returned it with another shrug.

"If that's what you want to do ..."

"Oh, stop being so polite!" Judy interrupted. "We'll do whatever you want."

"Now who's being polite?" Harry retorted.

They stared at each other across the table, but it might as well have been from across the continent.

"Sorry," Harry muttered.

"Me too."

Harry's hands and feet tingled with shock; she and Judy rarely fought. She didn't like all this anger and guilt, this jealousy and remorse. It hurt too much. "That bar sounds good. Let's go have a drink," she said gently, dropping a ten-dollar bill on the table.

Judy nodded and they both stood up. As they walked along the crowded sidewalk, Judy's hand slipped into Harry's. It was a gesture of trust, a small step on the path to reconciliation, and Harry accepted it. "I love you," Harry whispered fiercely, and was rewarded with Judy's first real smile of the day. The belief that the rest would come later gave her the courage to smile back.

It was only one in the afternoon, but the bar was busy. They found an empty table on the patio overlooking the water, ordered a jug of iced tea and alternated between staring out to sea and watching a foursome of women in their fifties dressed in denim play a spirited game of pool. Tame whitecaps broke lazily against the breakwater beneath them, and squawking seagulls dove for fish like careless pilots.

The sun was hot, the tea spiced and deliciously cold. Harry breathed in the ocean air, listened absently to desultory flirtations and the crack of cue on ball, and let the sunshine and the soothing rhythms of waves and warm voices of women lull her to a sleepy peacefulness. God knows she needed it.

"We should always live like this," Judy murmured.

"We should win the lottery," Harry answered with a laugh. She finished her tea and poured more.

"Never mind. People who are rich can't possibly appreciate what they have," Judy said.

"Well, I wouldn't mind finding that out for myself," Harry admitted.

"San Francisco in the spring."

"Provincetown in the summer."

"Bermuda in winter," Judy ventured.

"Naw — too cold. Try the Caymans," Harry suggested.

"Okay. The Caymans in winter. And a villa in France for the in-between times."

"A pool table in the basement," Harry mused.

"Aim higher."

"Right. How about a finished basement and then a pool table?"

"And a house to sit over it."

"In the suburbs."

"Or downtown."

"Both."

"Right. Dream on," Judy said with a stretch.

"But we could buy a house," Harry said slowly. "I mean, we're both working, we've got a little money in the bank ..."

One of the pool players whooped with triumph. Harry stopped talking and turned in time to see her wave her pool cue in the air.

Buying a house together was a big step. Maybe it was too soon. She thought of Lorna, of friends who were perhaps in the not so distant future to be considered as potential lovers, and gulped down tea, her peace of mind shattered like a fishing boat on a hidden shoal.

"Honey, don't."

Harry tried to smile but felt like crying.

"I feel wretched that I've hurt you so much."

"I'll get over it," Harry whispered, wondering if she would.

"Do you want to go for a swim?"

Harry felt prickly from the sun; her shorts and tee-shirt were damp with sweat. "That sounds good."

They retrieved Bug, lowered the windows to let the stifling heat out and drove back to the motel, changing into bathing suits while maintaining a carefully neutral banter. Harry shrieked as she plunged into the shockingly cold water, and then immediately dunked herself.

"God, I've never understood how you can do that!" Judy commented from shore when Harry surfaced. "It's so bloody cold!" she exclaimed, testing the water with a toe.

"Nova Scotians are tough. Besides, it only hurts for a minute," Harry said, turning over and floating on her back.

"That's what they all say!"

"You're such a coward!" Harry teased, standing up to splash water in her lover's general direction.

"Don't you dare!"

"Just trying to be helpful," Harry said saucily, flopping on her back again. She didn't have to allow Lorna to have meaning in her life, no more than she had to give her undivided attention to those wispy clouds trailing lazily across the sky. That one looked like a little puppy with its paw in the air. And the one on the left like the Duchess of York. And that one over there like a white rainbow pointing to the elusive pot of gold and if she had arms to reach that high she could embrace the universe and then Lorna wouldn't matter …

Fingers plucked at her toe; she lost her buoyancy and salt water filled her mouth. "Hey!"

"Make fun of me, would you?" Judy growled.

Harry stood up and spat water from her mouth. "You like to live dangerously, don't you?"

"Don't splash me!" Judy wailed, but it was too late. Harry's arms were circling, her hands scooping deep, then coming up fast. Water cascaded over Judy, who rushed forward through the maelstrom and grabbed Harry by the wrists.

"Kiss me, you nut!"

"Where, here?"

"Well, you can start with my lips," Judy laughed.

"But someone might see ..."

"So?"

Good question.

"Well ..."

"This is Provincetown, you dolt! Come on, give me a kiss!"

She did.

It was the first time Harry had ever got sunburnt in a bar, and of course it had to be there in Provincetown, where every lesbian in the universe was going to see her big, red nose. She combed her wet hair into submission and wondered if there was a hope in hell that it wouldn't start to peel before they got back to Montreal. She slapped the comb down on the counter and peered closely at her nose.

"I told you to wear sunscreen," Judy reminded her, stepping in front of the mirror to insert her earrings.

"But it was only for one drink," Harry complained. "And I nearly took a bath in suntan lotion before we went down to the beach."

"The ozone —"

"Aw, don't remind me," Harry interrupted, gingerly rubbing after-sun lotion on her face. Her dry skin ate it up. She applied another layer, determined to stop her nose from peeling.

Judy chuckled and walked away.

"Traitor," Harry called out.

The chuckle grew louder.

"Stop cackling!"

"Excuse me, but I never cackle," Judy sang out.

"You could have fooled me," Harry retorted, taking one last look at herself in the mirror. Her nose was now greasy as well as red.

"Stop feeling sorry for yourself and hurry up. I'm starving!"

"Me too," Harry agreed. She grabbed her bra and panties from the edge of the tub and left the bathroom.

"And you're not even dressed," Judy complained.

Harry's thoughts turned from food to something infinitely more close at hand when she saw the look on Judy's face. She walked over to the bed, plopped down beside Judy and kissed her.

"Harry, we'll be late," Judy said between kisses.

"Late for what?" Harry responded, gently pushing Judy back on the bed.

"I forget."

"Good. Vacations are for forgetting," Harry said, lifting her blouse and then slipping her shorts down over her hips. "And this."

"Oh, definitely that," Judy moaned as Harry's fingers slid under her panties and into the sweet wetness between her thighs. It was better than the night before. There was less tension. Judy stopped worrying about proving something to Harry, and Harry forgot about pretending that everything was all right, that nothing had changed. They were more playful; they teased each other, brought each other to the brink of orgasm and then stopped, retreated, retrenched, wanting to extend pleasure until it snapped like a rubber band stretched too tight.

"Oh, god!" Judy exclaimed, rolling over.

"It's the heat," Harry replied breathlessly.

"And here I thought it was me," Judy whispered.

"That too," Harry admitted gruffly. "That too."

"I'm famished," Judy said.

"You're insatiable."

"I'm talking about food, as you very well know," Judy retorted.

"And what was this?" Harry replied, swiftly reaching between Judy's thighs and unerringly finding her clit.

"You do that so well," Judy moaned.

"So does my tongue," Harry replied, moving down.

"Later, hon. Let's save it for later," Judy said. "Otherwise we'll never get anything to eat."

Harry reluctantly released her and sat up.

"I'm going to have to take another shower," Judy said. She walked into the bathroom and seconds later Harry heard the shower start. She got up and arranged the bedcovers and retrieved Judy's clothes from the floor, placing them neatly on the bed. She picked up her carry-all, pulled the crumpled newspaper from it and was about to toss it in the garbage can beside the bed when a headline written in small but bold type attracted her attention. "Missing Seashore Motel Owner Found Dead," it read.

"Oh my god," Harry muttered, sitting down on the bed. She smoothed out the sheet of newspaper with her hand and swiftly read the article:

" The body of Gertrude Cashin, 75, co-owner and manager of the Seashore Motel, West Yarmouth, was found yesterday in the living quarters behind the motel office by a guest attempting to check out. Ms. Cashin had been missing for over five years. Travelling salesman Clifford Jones of Toronto, Canada, who found the body, stated that Cashin had checked him into the deserted motel the day before. Police refused to comment further pending the results of an autopsy."

"I don't believe it," Harry whispered to herself.

"What?" Judy asked. She was naked except for a towel wrapped around her head, but Harry didn't notice.

"The owner of the motel I stayed in died," Harry said, rereading the article.

"No kidding!" Judy exclaimed, taking the newspaper from Harry. "Let me see."

Harry sighed. Poor Gertie; she had been old and frail, but vibrant and interested in life, if a bit eccentric. What a waste.

"But I don't understand," Judy said, handing the newspaper back to Harry. "It says here that she was missing for five years, and that the motel was deserted."

"Well, she wasn't missing when I got there," Harry replied. "She was alive and kicking and she took my money and invited me in for a drink. The motel wasn't deserted, either. There were at least two other cars in the parking lot." Gertie had also said some pretty bizarre things and sent her on an unproductive search for a restaurant which had been closed for years, but she didn't mention that to Judy. And later, when she got back from dinner, she had been certain that *there was no one there*. But that had just been her imagination.

"Maybe it wasn't her. Maybe it was somebody else," Judy suggested, sitting on the edge of the bed.

"But she said she was Gertrude Cashin," Harry said, plopping down beside her lover.

"People do lie, you know," Judy pointed out.

"Yes, but why would an elderly woman pretend to be somebody else?"

"Maybe she decided that it was a good way to make a few dollars and that nobody would ever know the difference, not as long as Gertrude Cashin was missing," Judy suggested.

"But lots of people in West Yarmouth must have known Gertrude Cashin. After all, it's a small town. If an imposter was running the motel, how could she be sure that one of her relatives or friends wouldn't come calling, or that an acquaintance wouldn't drop in?" Harry asked.

"It would have been quite a risk to take," Judy conceded. "So what do you think?"

"I don't know," Harry replied, completely baffled. "Perhaps she returned to the motel the night I got there and died after I checked in."

"That's quite a coincidence, but I suppose it's possible," Judy said. "But where was she during those five years? Had she been kidnapped?"

"I don't see how she could have been," Harry responded. "I mean, there she was, renting out rooms and socializing with her clients, or at least with me. If she invited me in for a drink, I suspect that she did the same thing with others. And she didn't seem upset or worried about anything."

"Which is not the typical reaction of a kidnap victim, is it? One would suppose that if she had been kidnapped, she would have gone straight to the police the minute she was released," Judy said.

"I don't know about you, but I certainly would have," Harry replied. "And I don't know why anyone would have kidnapped her in the first place, because I sure didn't get the impression that she had any money."

"Still, no matter where she was, it would be quite a coincidence for her to die the night she got back to the motel," Judy said.

"Maybe it wasn't the first night," Harry suggested.

"Perhaps not. She could have come back before. But that still doesn't explain where she was for five years," Judy said glumly.

"Maybe she had amnesia," Harry suggested. But somehow, she couldn't quite bring herself to believe it. Gertie was too vital, too alive, too *there* to have just recovered from a five-year bout of amnesia.

"But wouldn't she have gone to the police once she remembered who she was?" Judy argued. "And to tell the truth, I don't think all that many people suffer from complete amnesia, where they can't remember anything about themselves or where they came from, despite the number of television shows about it. It's a good story, something people can relate to. But how often does it happen in real life?"

"You're probably right. And if Gertie did have amnesia, she would most likely have been found wandering around," Harry said. "If you don't know who you are, it must be pretty hard to stay hidden."

"And wouldn't an amnesiac want his or her identity to be discovered?" Judy added. "Wouldn't they ask for help?"

"I suppose so," Harry said. "But what if she just decided to go off on her own?"

"And return to the motel five years later and start renting out units?" Judy replied, a puzzled look on her face.

"The place was run down. The furniture in Gertie's apartment and in my room hadn't been changed in years, and the office was unbelievably dusty. It made me sneeze," Harry said. "But my room was clean, and so was Gertie's apartment. So somebody was looking after the motel while she was gone. If she was gone."

"Do you think she went into hiding for some reason and made periodic visits to the motel to keep it clean and rent out units?" Judy asked.

"Look, the more we talk, the more confused I get. I just don't understand any of it," Harry replied. She looked at Judy, shivering as she remembered standing in the swirling fog and knocking on the door of the motel office, growing increasingly frightened with each passing second. Wherever she had been for the previous five years and whether she had returned that particular evening or some days before, Gertie had died the night Harry had stayed at the motel. And the question which neither she nor Judy had asked was whether she had died a natural death or whether she had she been murdered.

"It sounds really weird," Judy commented.

"You'd better believe it," Harry muttered, scanning the article for a third time. It was so frustratingly brief, so incomplete. She wondered how long the body had been there before Clifford Jones found it. Was it really Gertrude Cashin? Clifford Jones would have known if it had been the same woman who had checked him in. He would have been able to identify her. As could she. Perhaps she should call the West Yarmouth police and tell them she had stayed at the motel that night. She had signed the guest register, and if Gertie had been killed rather than dying a natural death, the police would probably be looking for her. Actually, they would likely be searching for her anyway; Gertie had been missing for five years, presumably under mysterious circumstances, and they would conduct a thorough investigation whether or not she had been murdered.

"Maybe I should call the police," she said to Judy.

The telephone rang.

"Why don't you take your shower and decide what you want to do?"

Harry carefully tucked the newspaper into her tote-bag and went into the bathroom. She reached down to turn on the shower, then paused when she heard Judy repeating the word "no," softly at first, then angrily. After a final "don't you dare!" Judy dropped the receiver with a crash.

"What was that all about?" Harry asked, craning her head around the corner.

"I'm paying for my mistake," Judy replied tersely. "Lorna wants to see me, and she doesn't want to take no for an answer. Hurry up and take your shower. I want to get out of here."

"But —"

"Please!"

Harry bit back her questions and turned on the shower. Less than five minutes later, she was dressed and ready to leave.

"You drive — I'm too angry," Judy said.

Just as Harry unlocked Bug, she heard tires squeal as a car rounded the corner and come barrelling up the driveway.

"Oh lord, it's her," Judy muttered.

"Lorna?" Harry asked.

"Who do you think? Gertrude Cashin?" Judy snapped. "Get in and drive!"

"Oh no, let's not confuse the two of *them*," Harry muttered, pushing the key into the ignition. Bug rumbled into life, and putting her in gear, Harry swiftly backed out of the parking lot and sped down the driveway just as the other car reached the top. Out of the corner of her eye she could see Judy ducking down in the seat, trying to make herself invisible.

Some vacation this has been, Harry thought dejectedly. "Why don't you just see her and get it over with?"

"What did you think I was trying to do this morning?" Judy snapped. "She wanted us to stay there. She thought we could be one big, happy family."

"You mean that's what you were arguing about?" Harry asked.

"Of course. What did you think? I tried to tell her that it just wouldn't work, but she was determined to inflict some of her wonderful hospitality on us."

"A fate worth than death," Harry muttered, only half in jest.

"Quite," Judy said with feeling. "I hope she isn't going to follow us."

"But she knows I'm here now, so why would she chase after you?" Harry asked, looking in the rearview mirror. There were cars behind Bug, but it was too dark to make out any distinguishing features.

"It's just another of her power games," Judy replied, her voice tired.

This was nuts, Harry thought. They were fleeing from a confrontation with a woman who sounded like what she needed more than anything was a good, firm "no." Or a kick in the seat of her pants. She slowed and pulled Bug over on the shoulder.

"What are you doing?"

"I'm going to turn around and go back to the motel," Harry replied.

"But —"

"If Lorna's there, we'll deal with her. She can't very well insist that we stay with her if I refuse, can she? And anyway, I don't think she'd bother to wait. She's probably on her way back to Provincetown by now," Harry answered.

"But we were going to have dinner," Judy protested.

"Are you still hungry?" Harry asked, reaching out and grasping one of Judy's hands. She heard Judy chuckle and knew that she wasn't the only one who had lost her appetite.

"Not really."

"Then let's head down the road," Harry suggested.

"And leave Provincetown? But you just got here," Judy protested.

"Judy, in case you haven't noticed, I'm not exactly having a good time," Harry said with deceptive lightness.

"It's all my fault," Judy said, withdrawing her hand from Harry's.

"Let's not go through all that again," Harry sighed. "Anyway, the main reason I want to leave is so I can go back to West Yarmouth and tell the police what I know."

"That's probably a good idea," Judy responded, "although you could call them."

"Yeah, I know. But getting out of here is probably the best thing for both of us right now, and West Yarmouth is on the way home."

Harry drove slowly through the dark, moonless night, leaving Provincetown behind. Judy soon drifted into a restless sleep in the seat beside her, and Harry fiddled with the radio, getting more static than music. She finally turned it off and drove in silence. Running away was not her usual way of dealing with problems; indeed, she was normally as tenacious as a terrier when faced with controversy, adversity or a sticky situation. But she had been determined to put some distance between herself and Provincetown, and soon, she hoped, between herself and Cape Cod. Her fragile equilibrium had been destroyed when she had read that frustratingly brief newspaper article. But even before that, she had felt uneasy about Gertie's bizarre behaviour, and she had been unsettled by the ominous mood and tenacious hold of that miserable dream. Whether she liked it or not, Gertie had made a strong impression on her, especially when, in her dream, Gertie had predicted problems in her relationship with Judy. Those predictions had come true, but perhaps there was nothing strange about that. She had been worried about Judy, she had been spooked by the deathlike stillness of the Seashore Motel, and her subconscious had likely put two and two together, resulting in her nightmare.

She was glad that Judy was asleep. It gave her the opportunity to think. Not that any amount of thinking was likely to clarify the situation, she thought wryly. There was too much she didn't know to be capable of understanding what was going on in her lover's life or in the life of a woman who had, if the newspaper article was correct, been missing for five years. Harry refused to believe that Gertie had been murdered, though, but not for any logical reason. She simply couldn't bring herself to believe that someone had been killed while she was sleeping in a motel room with nothing between her and a murderer but a flimsy door and an ill-fitting lock! Her death must have been accidental. Gertie had been drinking; perhaps she had fallen and hit her head on something and died. Or natural. She had been ill, so perhaps she had passed away in her sleep.

It was incredible that Gertie had been missing for five years. Her apartment looked — indeed, felt — lived in. There was a definite *presence* there, indefinable but nonetheless real. The Seashore Motel, while unkempt in appearance, had not been neglected. The rooms were clean, if shabby, hot and cold water flowed from the taps, and the light switches worked. Somebody had been paying the bills. It didn't make any sense. Still, it wasn't Harry's job to solve the mystery of her disappearance or subsequent death. That was up to the police.

And she had more immediate problems. She would have to stretch her emotional faculties to the limit to come to terms with the bombshell Judy had dropped today. It wasn't so much her temporary dalliance with an ex-lover; Harry was convinced that she could put that behind her once they got home. But it would be infinitely more difficult should Judy be determined to explore non-monogamy and to take other lovers, because she would be compelled to face the threat of permanent change in their relationship.

Why did Judy want to do this? If she loved Harry, which Harry was sure she did, why then was there this sudden need to go outside their relationship? Perhaps it wasn't sudden. Perhaps this was something which had grown in importance over time. Something which Harry hadn't noticed because she had grown complacent about their relationship and had started to take things for granted. She sighed and glanced at her lover. Judy's head was leaning against the window and her mouth was slightly open. She was going to have one hell of a stiff neck, Harry thought. Poor dear; she was obviously exhausted. She had certainly been determined to make a complete break with Lorna, and she'd been in a total snit when Lorna had refused to take no for an answer. When they had returned to the motel, Judy had thrown her clothes and toiletries into her suitcase with a speed which had amazed Harry, and while Harry had finished packing, Judy had insisted on sitting behind the wheel, ready to whip Bug into action the moment she spotted Lorna's car coming up the driveway. Talk about total avoidance! But when Judy made up her mind about something, she could be downright obsessive until she had seen it through.

As she had checked the dresser drawers for stray socks and the edges of the bathtub for overlooked bottles of shampoo, it had occurred to Harry that neither of them knew whether it had actually been Lorna's car which had chased them from the motel earlier that evening. Judy had been crouched down behind the dashboard, incapable of seeing either the car or Lorna, and Harry had been so intent on driving down the winding driveway without landing them in the ditch that she hadn't looked at the approaching car. Even if she had, she wouldn't have been able to identify Lorna through the glare of headlights. So maybe it had been a carload of somnambulant tourists returning to the motel after a sumptuous dinner in town. They must have been traumatized when Bug swung past them, moving like a bat out of hell, Harry thought, chortling to herself.

She sighed, slowed down and began looking for a motel with a vacancy sign.

"Where are we?" Judy asked sleepily, stretching.

"Around Hyannis Port," Harry answered.

"Already?" Judy exclaimed, sitting up.

"It's not all that far," Harry reminded her. "But I've been driving slowly, and it's late."

"We should stop and get some rest," Judy suggested.

"I've been looking, but all the motels are full," Harry said, taking one hand off the steering wheel to point to the "no vacancy" signs littering the landscape on both sides of the two-lane highway.

"Want me to drive, then?" Judy asked.

"In a minute," Harry said. "I've got to pee, so let me find a place to pull over, and then we'll switch."

They didn't locate a likely spot for a couple of miles. Harry's hunger had returned, and she thought longingly of the marvellous lobster lunch she had eaten in Wellfleet in that fishing shack by the water and of the dinner she and Judy had had in Provincetown. But only greasy spoons would be open this late at night, and she wasn't desperate enough to tamper with her digestive system.

"This looks like as good a place as any," Harry said, pulling Bug over and dousing the headlights. They took turns climbing down the slope into the deep gutter to relieve themselves, and then got back into the car.

"You wouldn't happen to have a stray chocolate bar hidden in the glove compartment, would you?" Judy asked.

"I don't think so," Harry replied, climbing into the passenger seat. She fastened her seat belt and rummaged through the glove compartment, finding her long-lost hairbrush and several rusty bridge tokens, but no food. "You're out of luck," she announced, cramming everything back into the glove compartment and closing the door as Judy pulled out onto the road.

"Turn off here," Harry said a few miles later.

Judy took the exit to West Yarmouth. "Where now?" she asked.

"I guess it's too late to go to the police station," Harry replied. "Let's keep looking for a motel, and I'll call them in the morning. Look, there's the Seashore Motel."

Judy slowed down. "The lights are on."

"And there's a car parked outside the office," Harry said.

"Do you think it's the police?" Judy asked.

"Who else would be there at this time of night?" Harry replied. "Do you want to go in?"

Harry shrugged.

"Let's. If it's the police, you can get it over with tonight," Judy urged.

While Harry was brooding, Judy flicked Bug's turn signal and turned into the driveway, parking Bug next to the other car.

Harry stared fixedly at the office, expecting to see the door open and Gertrude Cashin come swooping out, a registration form in one hand and a half-empty bottle of brandy in the other. But Gertie was dead, she reminded herself. No more perambulating, no more cryptic conversations, no more nips of brandy. Dead and gone. She looked around the deserted parking lot. There were no cars parked in front of any of the motel units, no lights on in any of the rooms. She watched a torn piece of newspaper blow across the courtyard and slide under Bug.

The office door opened, but it wasn't Gertrude Cashin who walked out, it was a tall, middle-aged man in a rumpled suit. Harry slumped down in her seat and watched him approach Bug. Judy rolled down the window.

"Mind showing me some identification?" he asked softly, flashing a badge.

Judy fumbled through her purse and took out her passport.

"And you?" he said to Harry, handing Judy's passport back to her.

Harry held out her passport for his inspection.

"Harriet Hubbley! We've been looking for you," he said with a tight smile.

"I thought you might be," Harry replied weakly.

"Why don't we continue this conversation in the office?" the police officer suggested. "You can leave your car here."

Judy turned off the ignition. They exchanged wan smiles, got out of the car and followed the police officer into the motel office.

"Let me see your passports again," he asked.

They handed them to him.

They sat on wooden chairs Harry had never seen before. The police officer removed a tattered notebook and ballpoint pen from his pocket, and opened their passports. Harry watched him slowly fill a page with carefully printed block letters. Then he closed their passports and handed them back.

She wished she wasn't there. She wished she had called instead of coming in person. She didn't like the police. Nothing personal, she was generally a law-abiding citizen whose only crime was to fail to come to a complete stop at stop signs and to speed on highways whenever Bug felt up to it. She was a typical Montreal driver, being otherwise would probably cause more accidents than it prevented. But she should give this cop the benefit of the doubt. Maybe he was a nice guy, maybe his mind was open, maybe he had a gay brother or sister or friend and didn't joke about ball-breaking bulldykes and limp-wristed fags over a beer with his buddies in the local cop bar. But the police were not exactly been the best friends of the gay and lesbian communities. More than one of her gay male friends had been arrested in bar raids in Montreal, and she had once been in a lesbian bar when several burly, hostile police officers had stormed in, turned on the lights and proceeded to do a head count and check IDs for underage women. So no, she didn't trust the cops.

"I didn't get your name," Harry said tentatively.

"Calvin."

"Calvin what?"

"John. John Calvin."

Don't say it, she warned Judy with a look. Do not say it. "Captain John Calvin," she hazarded. What she didn't know about police force nomenclature would fill a book.

"Detective Calvin," he corrected her without looking up, flipping to an empty page of his notebook. "Address, home phone number?"

Harry gave them.

"And you?" He asked, turning to Judy.

"The same," Judy said.

His expression didn't change. Harry decided that he was either too dumb to understand the implications, or smart enough to have realized that they were lesbians the minute he saw them. Fine, she thought. So he was either really dumb or really smart. That and a buck would get her a cup of coffee. Maybe.

"Profession?"

"Teacher," Harry replied.

He looked at Judy.

"Computer programmer," Judy told him.

"So you both stayed here?" the detective asked.

"No, just me," Harry responded.

"Where were you?" Calvin asked Judy.

"In Provincetown. I flew down nearly a week ago to visit with friends," Judy replied.

"So you were here alone," he said to Harry.

"Yes."

"Would you tell me what happened?"

"Well," she began, perching on the edge of the chair, and then she sneezed. The furniture in the office had been slightly rearranged, but dust still covered everything. "Look, I'm allergic to dust. Could we move into Gertie's apartment?" she asked between sneezes. "Otherwise, I probably won't be able to stop sneezing long enough to tell you anything."

"No," he said, shaking his head. "That's where the body was found, and we aren't quite finished with it yet."

Was he referring to the apartment, or to Gertie's body? They wouldn't leave her body there for very long, would they? Harry looked at the door to the apartment. It was closed, but she shivered anyway.

"I'm waiting, Ms. Hubbley," the police officer said with a sigh which he tried but did not entirely succeed in hiding.

Gertie's body must have been discovered soon after she had driven Bug down Route 6. While she was thinking about Judy, wondering about Judy, trying to put her nightmare and its depressing warning about Judy out of her mind.

She looked at Judy, then at the detective. She was tired. She was hungry. She needed a shower. But she would relinquish her claim to clean sheets, a good meal and a hot shower if she could avoid sitting in this dusty office and retracing her steps while this sleepy looking cop wrote down her every word for posterity ...

"Ms. Hubbley?"

"It was the night before last. I was on my way from Montreal to Provincetown, but it had been raining hard all the way from the border, so I decided not to drive after dark. I saw the sign and drove in to get out of the storm," Harry explained, pausing to find a tissue in her purse and blow her nose. "Gertrude Cashin was right there behind that counter."

Both Judy and Detective Calvin looked in the direction Harry was pointing. He made a note. Judy's expression was thoughtful. Harry sneezed and searched for another tissue.

"Alive," detective Calvin sighed.

"Well yes, what did you think I meant?"

"Never mind," he said dispiritedly. "That was your signature in the registration book, then," Calvin commented, writing something else in his notebook.

"Yes," Harry nodded, stifling a sneeze. Her nose was blocked, and her sinuses were beginning to ache. "Just after that of Clifford Jones."

"I've already questioned Mr. Jones," the officer said glumly. "He has been quite forthcoming."

Harry almost smiled and then thought the better of it. What Detective Calvin thought of Clifford Jones, travelling salesman, was probably better left unexamined. But from the detective's muted reaction, she deduced that Clifford had been unable to resist a mince or two in his direction. "And then Gertie — Ms. Cashin — invited me into her apartment for a coffee and some brandy," she continued.

"Back there?" The detective asked, his lethargy disappearing.

"Yes."

"How long were you in her apartment?"

"I'm not sure; I didn't look at my watch. But it was less than an hour," Harry replied, his sudden alertness making her feel uneasy. Did that make her a suspect? Gosh, maybe Gertie *had* been murdered. She took some time out and blew her nose.

"Do you know exactly when you arrived and when you left her apartment?" he asked as soon as she had dropped the soggy tissue into the outside compartment of her purse.

"Not really," Harry said. "I pulled into the motel around seven, I guess, and it was fairly dark when I got to the restaurant. But then again, it was raining and quite foggy, so it probably seemed later than it was."

"And precisely what did you do in Ms. Cashin's apartment?"

"We had coffee laced with brandy, chatted for a bit, and then Ms. Cashin gave me some advice on where to have dinner. I'd been driving all day, and I was quite hungry," Harry responded. She wondered whether to tell him how wildly erroneous Gertie's advise had been, how she had been sent to unearth a restaurant which was no longer open. She thought not.

"What did you talk about?" he asked, looking intently at her, as if he suspected that despite that fact that they were strangers, she and Gertie had divulged grand secrets or made a joint pact with the devil or something similar. Harry was tempted to give him what he wanted, but resisted. She knew that testimony about erroneous directions to a deserted restaurant where mice and other little critters were the only diners and a nightmare in which Gertie muttered about safe havens, dispensed rum by the tumbler and predicted the future with unsettling accuracy would not be credible.

"Oh, nothing much. I mean, we'd never met each other before, so she asked me what I did and then told me that she was retired," Harry replied.

"Did you know that Ms. Cashin had been missing for five years?" Calvin inquired.

"How could I have? I'd never been in West Yarmouth or anywhere else on the Cape before that night," Harry replied reasonably. "I didn't know about it until I read the article in the newspaper."

"And what did you think then?" he asked, making a note.

"I was surprised," Harry replied.

"How well do you know Clifford Jones?" Calvin asked abruptly.

Harry leaned back in her chair, feeling uncomfortable. "I don't know him at all," she answered.

"You weren't friends, or even acquaintances, back in Canada?" he persevered.

"The only time I ever saw him was yesterday morning when my car wouldn't start," Harry said, wondering if he was as abjectly ignorant of Canada's geography as the stereotypical Americans that Canadians told stories about — the ones who drove over the border during the summer months with skis attached to the top of their cars, and who stopped to ask where the polar bears were. But she couldn't believe that a police detective would be that ignorant; he was probably just doing his job by being suspicious about everything. "It was raining, and the dampness must have got into the engine. Clifford Jones came out to see if he could help, but the car started shortly after that, and I left for Provincetown. Actually, I think the two of us were the only ones there at that point."

"Do you remember how many cars were parked in the courtyard the night before last?" he inquired.

"Mine," Harry said immediately. "And two others."

"And in the morning?"

"Two, I believe."

"Were they the same cars as the night before?"

"I don't remember," Harry replied slowly.

"Are you sure?" he asked, sounding disappointed.

"It was foggy when I drove in that night, and I was really tired," Harry replied. "I wasn't paying much attention — I was just relieved to find a place to stay."

"I see."

"But I remember feeling surprised that the place looked so deserted," Harry added. "Especially in the middle of the tourist season."

Calvin stopped writing and glanced at her, his eyes sharp. "That's what Jones said."

"Well, that's the way it seemed," Harry said. "After passing so many 'no vacancy' signs, I thought it was strange that there weren't more people staying here. I probably wasn't the only person who got caught in the storm and didn't have a reservation."

"Let's go back a bit. Did you see Gertrude Cashin when you checked out?" he asked.

"No. It was early. I didn't want to disturb her. I just dropped my key through the mail slot in the office door and drove down to Provincetown. Didn't anyone find it?"

"Yes. Clifford Jones picked it up and put it on the counter. Ms. Hubbley, do you think you could identify Gertrude Cashin?" he asked.

"Do you mean —"

"No, no. Not the body. A picture," he interrupted, fumbling in his briefcase.

"Oh!" Harry exclaimed, embarrassed. "Of course."

"Here, then."

Harry took several large photographs from him.

"Which one is Gertrude Cashin?"

Harry looked swiftly through the photographs and found Gertie's halfway down the pile. A younger, plumper Gertie, but Gertie none the less.

"This one," she said, separating Gertie's picture from the pile and holding it out to him.

"You're sure," Calvin said after he had studied the photograph for several seconds.

Harry looked at him; he seemed to be chewing on his cheek.

"Very sure," Harry replied.

"I see," he muttered, taking the photograph of Gertie from her hand.

"Excuse me, detective, but what do you see?" Harry inquired, curiosity getting the better of her.

"I beg your pardon?"

"I said, what do you see?"

Calvin snapped his notebook shut and pocketed his pen. "I am not at liberty to disclose that," he replied.

Harry had never heard a police officer speak in such a prim voice. "But I don't understand," she complained. "I've answered all your questions, but I still don't know what's going on. You said that Gertrude Cashin was missing for five years; well, where did she go? When did she come back? And how did she die? Did she die in her sleep? Was she attacked? Murdered? Is that why the police are involved?"

"The police investigate every case of suspicious death," the detective replied swiftly, as if he was repeating something he had memorized from a police college textbook. He grew silent, chewed on his cheek for several seconds and then said, "I'd like you to stay in town overnight and come down to the station in the morning to make a statement."

Harry looked at Judy, who shrugged.

"Ten o'clock?"

"Fine," he said getting up. "We'll want to go through this with you again."

Oh great, Harry thought, standing up. Just what she needed. "Who should I ask for?"

"Me," Calvin said, stifling a yawn.

"Fine," she said, opening the door.

"Oh, and thanks for coming back," Calvin said. "It saved me having to track you down."

"You're welcome," Harry said dryly, letting the door close behind her.

"John Calvin?" Judy whispered as they walked across the courtyard to Bug. "Do you believe it?"

"It's no more fantastic than the rest of it," Harry replied.

Unfortunately, she thought as she put Bug in gear and sped along the blacktop searching for a motel with a room to let, unfortunately John Calvin was all too true. So much for idyllic vacations.

Harry was driving, and Gertie was fast asleep in the passenger seat. The fog was so thick that she could barely see the pavement. She lowered the window and stuck out her head, but the white line down the centre was fuzzy as a dissolving mirage. She would have to pull in somewhere or risk driving off the road.

She drove for miles but there were no side roads, no driveways, no flashing neon sign inviting the weary traveller to stop and stay awhile. She could see the spectre-like shapes of buildings looming over the road like an urban canopy of leafy branches, but all the buildings were dark. She was growing desperate. Salty rain water was running down her face, making her eyes sting, filling her mouth with bitter brine. She turned into the first driveway she had seen in miles, not caring where it led, and followed a narrow, rutted road which led to a litter-strewn parking lot.

"Wake up, Gertie, I've found a place," Harry said, getting out of Bug and staring up at the ramshackle building. There was a large, hand-painted sign across the sagging veranda, but she couldn't read the name through the fog.

"Goodness gracious, this has certainly changed since the last time I was here," Gertie exclaimed as she slammed the car door. "Why didn't you tell me?"

"I didn't know," Harry replied. "I don't live here, remember?"

"Of course you knew," Gertie said. "It's the Sea Shanty Restaurant. Why didn't you mention that it had fallen into such a state of disrepair?"

Harry opened her mouth and closed it again.

"Well?"

"Shhh — it's late and we don't want to wake anybody," Harry whispered, trying to change the subject. She took a step forward.

"It doesn't appear to be very lively, does it?" Gertie said, "although the front door is ajar. Come on, let's go in. I'm ready for a feed of clams and a good night's sleep."

If it was as deserted as the real Sea Shanty Restaurant had been, there wouldn't be any clams to eat or beds to sleep in, but Harry stilled her tongue and followed Gertie up the creaking stairs and through the front door.

"Mmmm. Smell that?" Gertie asked.

Harry paused inside the door and sniffed. The malignant odour of damp plaster, infested wood and rotting garbage curled her nose.

"Smells good, doesn't it? Freshly baked bread, steamed lobster — all we have to do is find the dining room and we'll be in rolling in clover," Gertie announced. "Come with me."

Gertie took her hand and led her through a rabbit warren of long corridors and empty rooms. Harry stumbled in the dark and clung to Gertie. She certainly didn't want to get lost or to be abandoned here.

"There! What did I tell you?" Gertie said as she opened a door.

Harry blinked, her eyes smarting from the bright light. The wood-panelled dining room was eerily silent, but the tables were set. The tablecloths were a brilliant white, and the flatware sparkled. The scent of freshly baked bread and a variety of seafood assailed her senses. The restaurant was devoid of patrons, but several waiters were at work, refolding a napkin here, straightening a knife or fork there.

"How did this get here?"

Gertie just smiled.

"A table for two?" asked the maitre d'.

"Certainly," Gertie replied.

He seated them at a table overlooking the formal gardens, which were lit by artfully placed floodlights.

"This is all wrong," Harry whispered as the waiter placed an enormous platter of steamed clams in the middle of the table.

"We did want clams, didn't we?" Gertie said.

"That's not what I meant!"

"Calm down and have a clam, Harriet," Gertie commanded. "And take a drink of wine. It's good for the digestion."

Harry was hungry. She gave up and ate. The clams seemed real. So did the wine. And the crusty bread.

"You know, it wasn't easy to be a lesbian in those days. There were all kinds of laws. Well, you can always break the law, or simply ignore it, especially if it isn't a good law. Which this one definitely wasn't. Society was different then, though; more closed off, more rigid. You were required to be what people expected you to be. You were bred for a purpose, and becoming a homosexual was certainly not a fulfilment of that purpose. People didn't want to know that you were gay; they didn't even want to suspect it, or to guess. You had to hide it, to pretend to be like the rest of them. Of course, it was the moral condemnation, being labelled as a pervert, the assertion that you were engaging in unnatural acts which kept most of us in the closet and turned the rest into outcasts. The pressure of relatives and friends and of society itself overwhelmed us, made us deny ourselves, and often pushed us into a life we hated. You were either a sinner, or you were sick. Or both," Gertie said, carelessly tossing an empty clam shell into a bowl.

"I guess it was difficult," Harry replied, buttering another piece of bread.

"I knew I was a homosexual from a very young age. I suffered from terrible crushes on older women, and fell in love with half my female classmates. Boys were fun to play with, they liked the rough-and-tumble games I enjoyed, but once we grew older, they became irrelevant. But Vera, my darling Vera was never sure, although it was plain as the nose on your face that she was a lesbian through and through," Gertie said. "But then, you never met her, so you'll just have to take my word for it."

"Certainly," Harry replied, removing another clam from its shell and popping it into her mouth. The clams, steamed in a white wine sauce with just a hint of spiciness, were delicious; she would have to tell Judy about this restaurant when she woke up.

"The problem with Vera was that she didn't want to be different. She was a conventional sort of person, and under other circumstances, she would have been content to follow the straight-and-narrow path, straight being the operative word, of course. I courted her ever so gently, and we fell in love. It took a long time for her to admit it, but she finally did," Gertie said with a smile.

"Good for you," Harry said, concentrating on the clams.

"Yes, well, temporarily it was," Gertie replied, filling their wine glasses from a bottle which had appeared on the table while Harry wasn't looking. "We became lovers, and I was delirious as a bee in a rose. We didn't live together, though. I had an apartment and lived alone, which was considered quite risqué by everyone, including my parents. Young women were supposed to live at home with their parents until they married, unless they were going off to study nursing or education, that is, in which case they were herded like compliant sheep into a residence, or they were boarded with respectable families. None of that for me, though; I had no intention of going from one prison to another. At least I knew how to manipulate my parents, an advantage I would have lost had I put myself at the mercy of some starched senior nurse or some couple who believed that their responsibility to protect the virtue of the young woman staying with them was a sacred trust. No, I was a determined little lady in those days, and I generally got what I wanted."

"That hasn't changed much," Harry said, amused by Gertie's pleased expression.

"You'd better believe it," she said. "Vera lived at home with her parents, which was not the ideal situation. I was impatient. Once we became lovers, I wanted her with me all the time. You know how it is. I was young and horny, and I didn't want to waste any of it."

Harry nodded.

"Come to think of it, that was one thing I didn't outgrow as I got older," Gertie said with a laugh. "You only live once, you know, so you have to get what you can when you can."

Harry nodded again.

"But I'm getting off the track. I had a little money, a small inheritance from my grandmother, and chanced upon the idea of going into business," Gertie explained as the waiter removed their plates. "Shall we have more clams?"

Harry was indecisive.

"No? Another bottle of wine, then," Gertie suggested.

"Well…"

"I know — bring us two brandies, your best, mind you," she told the waiter.

"What happened?" Harry asked.

"Vera also had a little money, so after a lot of hemming and hawing and interference from her father, we finally bought the motel," Gertie said, lifting the brandy snifter and holding it up to the light.

"And?"

"Vera was so young. Oh, we were close in age, but she was such a child emotionally. I suppose I should have known better, but I didn't. I asked her to move into the motel with me. That had been my intention all along, and I thought her parents would acquiesce gracefully because the motel had been allowed to go to seed and needed a lot of work to make it commercially viable. There were so many things to be done, and it would have been more convenient and essentially quite normal for both owners to live there. But no. She wouldn't. This state of affairs went on for two or three years, so you can imagine how frustrated I became."

"Her parents wouldn't let her?"

"*She* wouldn't let *herself*," Gertie replied. "She was afraid people would *talk*. I didn't give two hoots about that, people in small towns always talked. They did then, and they do to this day. It's human nature, and vicious to the nth degree. If you didn't get married, they chattered about what a tragedy it was. People were suitably sympathetic at first, but before you knew it, all that brutal backbiting started. They wondered what was wrong with you. Were you so forward or so intelligent that you scared off the men? Were you so plain that nobody wanted you? Or were you so shy or so dumb that you couldn't hold a man, or so beautiful that you scared them away?" Gertie said.

"Things haven't changed all that much," Harry remarked, thinking about her home town.

"And then if you married the wrong person, they prattled on about how miserable you must be. If you didn't have any children, they dissected your sex life. Or, rather, your sex organs to see what could possibly be wrong with them. If you had too many children, everyone privately thought that your husband was oversexed and wouldn't leave you alone. Women themselves weren't supposed to have an interest in sex. And heaven help you if you flirted too much with a man who was not your husband or drank too much in public or did any one of an inordinate number of things which were considered verboten! Reputations, like Rome, could be lost in a day," Gertie said.

"It sounds horrible," Harry commented.

"Doesn't it, though? But there were ways to buck the system, to get around it, and I became familiar with most of them. But Vera didn't want to know. She suffered from fits of anxiety every time we were together. Getting her to take her clothes off was a major step. Having a little snooze in bed after was virtually impossible. She was afraid someone would come snooping and find us in a compromising situation. I was willing to take the chance, but she was petrified of being found out. Of being ruined, ostracized. She said it would kill her, and now I think it might have, but I wasn't listening then. I thought she would change, that she would grow accustomed to the need for secrecy and subterfuge, that she would eventually develop a cloak and dagger mentality. But she never did. I was impatient. I accused her of not really wanting to be with me when the real problem was her inability to deal with the situation. We had grown up together, so I should have known better. She was miss-goody-two-shoes right through school, always well behaved, anxious to please our teachers, to conform to the status quo. I should have realized that she wasn't going to change. It would have been better if we had moved away, if we had joined the anonymous crowds in the city and slowly surrounded ourselves with a circle of friends we could trust. Here, everyone knew her, and she was constantly being barraged with questions about when she was going to get married. Of course I was in the same position, but I didn't care. I gave up any pretence of being interested in the latest fashions, dating, house parties, men, and let people think what they would. Small towns always had old maids, after all, and I knew that as I got older, people would lose interest. But Vera couldn't bring herself to make that final break, so she continued to see men," Gertie said.

"That must have been difficult for you," Harry said, sipping her brandy.

"Oh, it was. I was jealous. There were scenes. I put too much pressure on her, and the next thing I knew, she was on her way to California to stay with relatives for the summer. An uncle, I believe. Her mother told me that she was simply exhausted from her responsibilities at the motel, and that the doctor had ordered a complete rest. Huh! A complete rest! Vera was as healthy as a horse. No, I knew at once that she was running away from me."

"And?" Harry asked after a long pause during which Gertie finished her brandy and waved her empty snifter at the waiter, who was hovering nearby.

"While she was in California, she met a man and married him," Gertie replied. "He was quite a bit older than her, a handsome fellow, I heard, although I could never tell a good-looking man from a homely one."

"No!" Harry exclaimed. She was shocked.

"Here, finish your brandy. He's bringing us another," Gertie told her.

"She got *married*?"

"She got married and never came back. And she returned my letters unopened," Gertie said.

"And you waited for her all these years?" Harry asked.

Gertie obviously didn't want to answer that particular question, Harry thought as mist clouded her eyes. When it dissolved, she was standing in front of an oversized easy chair in Gertrude Cashin's living room with a brandy snifter in her hand. The fog swirled around the lamp in the corner like a moth attracted to light.

"Sit down, Harriet, before you fall down!" Gertie said, emerging from the outer office. "Sometimes I think that you youngsters don't understand anything. The generation gap drives me crazy sometimes," she muttered, sipping from her brandy snifter.

"But — but what happened to the restaurant?" Harry asked, bewildered.

"Oh, don't worry, I paid the bill," Gertie replied. "Why don't you sit down?"

Since Gertie's nose was only an inch from hers, Harry sat.

"That's better. Now finish your drink before you go," Gertie said with a smile.

Harry obeyed and took a sip, choking on the rum. Oh lord; rum after brandy after wine. She was going to have a spectacular headache when she woke up. But she was getting used to warm rum. And the more rapidly she emptied her glass, the quicker she would be able to wake up and get on with the rest of her life. But it was not to be; even as she drained the last drops of rum from the brandy snifter, Gertie was refilling it straight from the bottle.

"I think I've had enough," Harry said politely, and then she burped.

"Ah, now there hangs a tale," Gertie said.

"Don't be naughty," Harry chastised her, and then, astonished by what she had said, she put her hand over her mouth and giggled.

Gertie laughed.

Spiffed. She was well and truly spiffed. But if Gertie didn't care, then Harry didn't either. And getting drunk was certainly a good way to synchronize the thickening fog in the room with the haze seeping into her mind, she thought wryly, taking another drink.

"Well, are you ready to hear the rest of the story, or not?"

"Huh?"

"The story, Harriet, the story! Are you completely without curiosity, without imagination?"

She wondered whether Gertie would go away if she ignored her, if she would disappear in a puff of smoke, dematerialize into the fog, snake away like that tendril which was reaching out to tickle her nose…

"Hey!"

Gertie roared with amusement. "Had to get your attention somehow, didn't I?"

The tendril withdrew. Harry decided that she hadn't seen it anyway. Too much rum did funny things to her vision, that was all.

"I don't think you're ready," Gertie said, suddenly serious again. "Not yet."

"But …"

"Soon."

Harry responded by finishing the rum in her brandy snifter. Lord, she was drunk! She closed her eyes.

"Don't fall asleep," Gertie warned.

Silly. She *was* asleep.

"Harriet!"

Harry opened her eyes and looked around the room. The fog had disappeared, as had Gertie. The lamp in the corner was burning bright, hurting her eyes. Harry stood up and looked behind the chair, but Gertie wasn't there. She went out into the office, but Gertie wasn't there either. If she hadn't had so much to drink, she would be able to think. And to find Gertie. She opened the door to outside and the fog rushed in.

"Now see what you've done."

"Sorry," Harry apologized, closing the door. But the damage had been done; fog surrounded her with such alacrity that Harry imagined it was alive and seeking the warmth of her body. She walked back to Gertie's apartment on feet she couldn't see. It was disconcerting, but she was not particularly surprised. "Do you mind if I help myself to another drink?" she asked politely.

There was no response.

There was no rum bottle, either. Just fog. Boring, Harry thought, and then she woke up.

Her body was awash with sweat and she felt as drunk as she had been in her dream. Nightmare, she corrected herself, wishing her dreams of Gertrude Cashin would cease and desist. She threw off the covers and heard Judy grunt in her sleep, and then she knew where she was. In the Shoreline Motel in West Yarmouth, across the road from the Seashore Motel.

Harry got out of bed, telling herself that she wasn't really suffering from a hangover, that too many drinks imbibed in a nightmare couldn't possibly leave her foul-mouthed and headachey when she woke up. She walked over to the window and peeked through the curtains, not surprised to see her face reflected in the fog. It was raining, too.

Harry sighed, let the curtains fall back into place and slid under the covers. She was exhausted. These dreams of Gertie left her confused, enervated. There were never any answers, just more questions. And the story Gertie had been telling her about Vera, was that true? How could she find out? With the exception of Detective Calvin, she didn't know anybody in West Yarmouth, and she was certainly not going to ask *him*. And even if she did manage to corral a local, would she have the nerve to pose the question? To casually inquire whether a young woman named Vera whose family lived in the vicinity had gone out west on vacation forty or fifty years ago and married a Californian? She could pretend she was a historian working on a book about the area or a sociologist researching the east-west migrating patterns of Americans. But what if it was true? What if Vera was a *real person*?

She sat up, her spine rigid with shock. That was enough, she told herself. She was having nightmares, nothing more. Gertrude Cashin was dead. She retrieved her watch from the bedside table and squinted at it. "Judy, you'd better wake up," she said, turning on the lamp.

Judy groaned and rolled over on her back, but her eyes stayed shut.

"We've got exactly thirty minutes to get down to the police station," Harry announced, pulling her nightgown over her head and tossing it on the bed.

"Oh, god," Judy moaned. One eye half-opened, then closed.

"Wake up," Harry said again. "I'll take my shower and then you can get in."

Both eyes opened this time and stayed open, although they weren't focussed. Harry went into the bathroom. She didn't want a shower, she wanted to get dressed, throw her stuff in her suitcase, crank up Bug and go home to their airy, walk-up apartment in downtown Montreal. She wanted to sleep in her own bed, not on some strange-smelling mattress in a motel room. She wanted to eat food she had cooked herself and not limp salads or greasy hamburgers or even gourmet lobster. She wanted to forget she had ever met Gertrude Cashin, obliterate the Seashore Motel from memory, dream sweet dreams and not nightmares which made her feel like she was plodding through molasses.

So you can't always have what you want, Harry reminded herself as she got out of the shower and held open the curtain while Judy stepped in. The steam reminded her of fog which reminded her of things she did not want to remember.

They dressed in silence, then agreed to brunch later, after.

"We're going to be late," Judy said, glancing at her watch as they left the room.

Harry unlocked Bug, slid in, and reached across to open the door on the passenger side. "I don't think John Calvin will arrest me for that."

Judy snorted. "John Calvin. Do you think anybody has told him?"

"He's probably been told so many times that he gets suspicious when he isn't," Harry replied.

"Just like a cop," Judy laughed.

"We shouldn't typecast him," Harry warned.

"Of course not," Judy agreed, "but do you think he knows?"

"How could he not know?" Harry asked.

"Easily," Judy said. "What if his family wasn't religious?"

"Do you think a name like that just flew in the window?" Harry said, raising her eyebrows.

"Stranger things have happened," Judy replied.

"True." Harry said. "But it would be just my luck if this cop is a straight-laced puritan who hates gays."

"Hey, policemen get around," Judy said reassuringly. "And this is Cape Cod, after all. I'm sure he's seen a lesbian or two in his time."

"Right," Harry said. But she wasn't convinced. "I still feel strange."

"Well, it's not every day that you get questioned by a police officer. But don't worry. You had nothing to do with any of this, you just happened to be in the wrong place at the wrong time. We'll be home soon, anyway," Judy said, patting her shoulder.

Harry could hardly wait.

The police station was just like all the police stations Harry had seen on television, only worse. It smelled like a men's locker room in mid-season, the walls were painted a bile yellow, faded in places and flaked in others, and the strong odour of disinfectant wafting up from the floor bit into her nose.

"I have an appointment with detective Calvin," Harry said to the harried looking uniformed policewoman sitting behind a battered desk.

"Take a seat," she said, gesturing to several mismatched chairs lined up against the far wall.

They sat down. Harry watched the policewoman pick up a phone, speak into it, grin, and then hang up. She hoped Calvin wasn't going to keep them waiting, because she was starving. Neither she nor Judy had eaten anything since their croissant and coffee brunch the day before, and being a three-squares-a-day type of woman, she was beginning to experience severe hunger pangs.

"Good morning, Ms. Hubbley, Ms. Johnson," John Calvin said. He had a different suit on today, but it was just as rumpled as the one he had been wearing the night before. Harry wondered absently whether he preferred them that way or whether his salary didn't cover the cost of dry cleaning.

"Good morning," Harry replied, clearing her throat.

"If you'll just come with me," he said politely.

"Certainly," Harry replied, and both she and Judy stood up.

"Just Ms. Hubbley, if you don't mind," Calvin said to Judy.

Harry was stricken. "But —"

"I'd prefer to see you alone, Ms. Hubbley," Calvin said. "Your friend wasn't there, after all."

"All right," Harry agreed, reluctantly.

"You can wait here if you like," he told Judy, "or come back in an hour."

Judy nodded and gave Harry an encouraging smile. "I'll go have a bite to eat," she said, "and meet you back here later."

"Okay," Harry replied, her mouth filling with saliva at the thought of food. "Why don't you scout out a place for lunch while you're at it?"

"You've got it."

Harry followed the detective down a long corridor, up a narrow flight of stairs and into a small, stuffy office which was crammed with two enormous metal desks, four battle-scarred filing cabinets and several wood chairs. The lone window was tiny, coated with soot, and looked as if it hadn't been opened since the police station had been built. The hardwood floor was worn down to the nails, their tiny heads shining with the polishing of years of constant traffic.

"Have a seat," Calvin said, gesturing to the most uncomfortable wood chair Harry had ever seen. She sat in it anyway and watched Calvin pick up a phone and mutter something into it.

The door opened and a policewoman walked in.

"This is Officer Yokes," Calvin announced. "She'll be taking notes. After the interview, she'll type them up and then I'll ask you to read the statement and if it's correct, to sign it. Is that clear?"

Harry stared at Officer Yokes, who was simply gorgeous. She always did have a weakness for women in uniform. They invariably looked attractive to her — butchy but attractive — although experience had taught her that appearances could be embarrassingly deceptive. Women in uniform could be just as vacuous, just as dumb and just as mean as women out of uniform. But still, she could enjoy herself looking, there was nothing wrong with that.

"Is that clear?" Calvin repeated.

Harry nodded and wrenched her eyes away from Officer Yokes. Wasn't there something else, though? "Don't you have to read me my rights first?" she inquired in a thin voice.

Calvin looked up, obviously amused. "You're a witness, Ms. Hubbley, not a suspect."

"Oh."

"Unless you have something to tell us which you think might incriminate you," he added. Harry supposed he couldn't resist.

"Not at all," she hastened to say.

"Fine."

"I just wasn't sure how it went," she added, feeling stupid. She had got off on the wrong foot, she thought glumly, glancing with embarrassment at Officer Yokes, who was busy scribbling on a steno pad. The problem was that even when she knew she had done nothing wrong, she still *felt* guilty. Presbyterian angst, Judy called it, although Harry protested she hadn't been brought up Presbyterian. Judy said it didn't matter, it was the same thing. But then, Judy hadn't grown up in a small Nova Scotian town which preached the work ethic from cradle to grave. Idle hands, etc. And idle minds were even worse. You were presumed guilty until you were found innocent. Actually, it sounded just like the West Yarmouth Gertie had described in her dream. But never mind. Judy (and Gertie, Harry was sure) had never suffered from this moral conundrum. She always knew for certain whether she was guilty or not, and when she wasn't, she didn't waste time or energy worrying for nothing. In contrast, some days Harry was positive that she was the cause of all the world's ills, that it was her fault her students knew nothing and what was worse, couldn't care less that they were fated to live their lives in ignorance. Judy maintained that this tendency of Harry's was not only conceited, it was as useless and debilitating as a diseased appendix. Still, Harry didn't know how to get rid of it.

"Fine, then. We'll start," Calvin said, flipping through his tattered notebook.

He took Harry through her drive from Montreal to the Cape, her arrival at the Seashore Motel, her coffee and conversation with Gertrude Cashin, her lobster dinner, her brief chat with Clifford Jones the following morning, her drive to Provincetown and what she had done there. He went on to closely question her about what she and Gertie had discussed, and Harry enlarged on what she had told him the night before, artfully abridging their conversation, of course. She didn't mention Gertie's inexplicable emphasis on the Seashore Motel being a haven in the storm. And she left out the part about Gertie being a lesbian. It was none of his business, and besides, she didn't want any official records of her own lesbianism to exist, not in a country where acts between consenting adults of the same sex were still thought to be unnatural and even illegal in many states of the union. She wasn't sure about Massachusetts. Not that it mattered; she was going to do what she normally did in her bed (and elsewhere, for that matter), laws be damned.

She was troubled, though; she had given Calvin the bare-bone details about her arrival on the Cape and her inadvertent involvement in Gertie's death, but she couldn't tell him about the most important things — her persistent impression that there was something not quite right about the Seashore Motel, intimations of Gertie's strangeness, her anxiety about Judy as she had driven down the highway. And then there were her nightmares. But they were probably the result of an over-active imagination, and even if she did mention them to Calvin, he wouldn't take them seriously. Worse yet, he might think that she was neurotic.

"And you don't know anything else," Calvin said.

"Like what?" Harry said, too tired and hungry to worry about being polite.

"Like where Gertrude Cashin was during the past five years," Calvin said.

"Do you think *I* had anything to do with her death?" Harry said incredulously.

"I didn't say that," he replied, "although you might have been the last person to see her alive."

That shocked her. But why was Calvin giving her the third-degree if she wasn't suspected of anything? Was this Calvin's natural style? And why wouldn't they tell her how Gertie had died, whether she had expired from natural causes or whether she had been murdered? The hair on the back of Harry's neck rose. "That was a coincidence," she croaked. She began to sweat profusely.

"Calvin, she's going to pass out," Yokes warned.

"Shit!" Calvin jumped up and pried open the window.

What did she mean? Of course she wasn't going to faint, Harry protested, although no words came out. An odd haze misted her eyes.

"Here. Put your head between your legs," Yokes counselled.

Harry felt a warm hand on the back of her neck push her down.

"Try to breathe normally," Yokes told her.

"It's just that I haven't eaten since brunch yesterday," Harry said apologetically, blinking rapidly to clear the haze.

"Would you like some coffee?" Yokes asked.

"Yes."

"I'll get it," Calvin said eagerly.

"Pick up a sandwich too," Yokes suggested.

"Right."

Harry heard the door close. The haze was receding; she could see the dirty floor under her sandals. "I feel okay now," she said to Yokes.

The hand disappeared from the back of her neck and she sat up. "I take it he doesn't like fainting women," she joked.

Yokes shrugged uncomfortably and turned away.

"It's just that I'm hungry," she said, trying to reassure the policewoman. And herself.

"You looked as pale as a ghost," Yokes commented, picking up her pencil and steno pad.

"Well, if he was trying to shock me, he certainly succeeded," Harry said caustically.

"That's for sure," Yokes replied, smiling briefly.

If Officer Yokes wasn't a dyke then neither was she, Harry decided. "I've been up here a long time — I'm hope my lover isn't getting worried," she said, looking directly at the policewoman.

"I'm sure she'll be all right," Yokes replied, her stare anything but casual. "There's a coffee machine down there, although the chairs aren't too comfortable."

It had been a big step to take. Harry could have declared that Officer Yokes had insulted her and made a complaint. Or she could have tittered, claimed that there had been a misunderstanding, and denied all. Or Officer Yokes herself could have refused to take the bait. Of course, they could still continue to ignore their attraction to each other.

"It's tough," Yokes said.

"Yes, it is," Harry replied, not knowing or caring whether Officer Yokes was referring to her own career as a police officer, to Gertrude Cashin's death, or to being a lesbian. Or to the difficulties inherent in being a cop and wanting to make a pass at someone you're questioning.

"Here we are. Three coffees and one sandwich," Calvin announced, kicking the door closed. "I hope you like tuna — it was all they had left," he added.

"That's just fine," Harry lied. She hated tuna.

"Feeling better?" Calvin asked after he was seated in the chair behind his desk.

"Much," Harry answered, holding her breath and biting into the tuna sandwich, then washing it down with a gulp of incredibly hot, strong and not particularly good coffee. She resigned herself to not sleeping that night, should she live until then; chances were that she would expire from caffeine overdose long before she went to bed.

"Sorry I came on so strong," Calvin said gruffly.

"That's quite an understatement," Harry said evenly.

He had the good grace to look embarrassed.

"Can I ask you something?"

He grunted.

"Gertrude Cashin was missing for five years, right?"

Calvin grunted confirmation again without looking up.

"And nobody knew where she was until she turned up dead in her apartment in the motel," Harry continued.

The cop of a thousand grunts, Harry thought sourly.

Calvin finally looked at her. "That's about it, Ms. Hubbley," he said tiredly. "Nobody seems to have known that she came back to the motel except for you and Clifford Jones. She checked him in about an hour before you arrived, and then you had coffee with her. Apparently no one saw her after that. The next morning, Mr. Jones went to the office to check out. From what you've told us, I gather that this was shortly after you drove off. It was early, anyway, since he had decided to check out before having breakfast. He knocked on the door, but there was no answer. He thought to try the door, which was open, so he went in. The outer office was empty, but the door to Ms. Cashin's apartment was ajar, so after calling her name a couple of times, he became concerned that she was ill, or had had an accident, so he went looking for her. He found her in one of the easy chairs."

"The one next to the lamp?" Harry asked with a shiver. Hearing about it from Calvin in such a dispassionate voice was disconcerting.

"Drink some more coffee," Yokes said curtly.

Harry gave her a grateful look and did as she was ordered.

"No, the other easy chair, the one just inside the door," Calvin replied.

"How did she die?" Harry asked, her voice trembling.

"Would you like another coffee?" Yokes said anxiously.

"No, thanks," Harry answered, smiling at her. She was practically certain that she wasn't going to faint again.

"There was an empty bottle of pills on the table beside the chair," Calvin replied, finishing his coffee.

"Pills?"

"Painkillers," he clarified. "Ms. Cashin had been battling breast cancer for years. It had spread, and according to her doctor, it was terminal."

"She was missing for five years, nobody knows whether she had any medical treatment for cancer during that time, and yet she only died two nights ago?" Harry asked incredulously. "Wouldn't she have had to find a doctor, even if it was just to renew her prescription?"

"We don't know the answers to those questions yet," Yokes said rather sharply.

"Although we're certainly checking into them," Calvin said.

Harry had the feeling he was lying, or at least exaggerating.

"I do agree with you about one thing, though. According to the doctor, she must have been in incredible pain, so I imagine she found someone to provide her with painkillers," Calvin added.

"Any fool knows that that's not hard to do," Yokes scoffed.

Calvin gave his subordinate a stern look; she bent assiduously over her notebook.

"So you think she died of an overdose," Harry said.

Calvin nodded.

"But she didn't seem like the type. She was so energetic, so talkative, so interested in life," Harry protested, remembering the frail but alert Gertrude Cashin who had loaned her a towel, signed her in, taken her money and plied her with much better coffee than the police station had likely ever percolated. The Gertrude Cashin who had talked about an absent lover in California, offered her a second brandy, and revealed her own lesbianism.

"Terminal illness can force people to make difficult choices," Yokes said quietly. "So can pain."

"The doctor told her she didn't have long to live, and that was five years ago. It was a miracle she held out for as long as she did. The medical examiner said her whole body was filled with cancer. He didn't know how she was still alive," Calvin said soberly.

"I see," Harry said. She had realized that Gertie was sick, but not that sick. She wished that she had skipped dinner, stayed for a second brandy and kept her company for a little longer. But she hadn't known, she couldn't have known.

"I've only got a couple more questions," Calvin said. "You said you had a brandy in her apartment that night."

"I had coffee with brandy in it," Harry confirmed.

"And Ms. Cashin?"

"She had the same thing."

"What was it served in?"

"A mug," she said.

"Where did you put yours when you left?"

"On the table beside the chair," Harry replied. "Did you find it there?"

"There was an empty mug on the table by her chair, and an open bottle of brandy next to it. There was a second empty mug on the table by the other chair. The coffee pot was still plugged in, and a dirt-streaked white towel was draped over one of the kitchen chairs," he told her.

"That must have been the towel Gertie gave me," Harry said. "I got soaked running from the car to the office when I checked in."

"There was also some cash in the till in the office," he added.

"It was probably mine. I paid her in cash," Harry said.

"It seems pretty clear to me," Calvin said. "She must have taken the pills soon after you left."

Harry looked away. There were tears in her eyes and she struggled to overcome a sense of guilt she shouldn't be feeling. She hadn't known.

"Well, thank you," Calvin said somewhat formally, rising from his chair.

"But — but what happens now?" Harry asked.

"Officer Yokes will call you when your statement is typed up and ready to sign," he replied.

"I have to come back here?" Harry asked, unable to keep the dismay from her voice.

"I'm afraid so," Calvin said rather dryly, the hint of a smile cracking one corner of his mouth.

"I'll call you," Yokes said. "But don't sit around and wait," she added swiftly. "I've got a few other things to finish before I get to this, so I'll leave a message as soon as it's ready."

"You mean I might have to stay another night?" Harry said slowly, looking from Yokes to Calvin.

He shrugged. "It depends."

Harry didn't ask on what; she supposed that police bureaucracy creaked as slowly as any other. She sighed. "And what about Gertie?"

"Oh, the lab will do some more tests, but that's about it," Calvin replied.

"I see," Harry said, and she did. As soon as the autopsy report confirmed what the police already believed, the case would be closed, and the file would be tucked away in the back of a bottom drawer. Gertrude Cashin, suffering from advanced and terminal cancer, had taken her own life.

And yet.

And yet. Where had Gertie been for the last five years of her life? Didn't they want to know? Didn't they care?

"Officer Yokes will show you out," Calvin said, extending his hand.

Harry shook it and followed Yokes from the room.

"Is he always like that?" Harry asked once the door was closed.

"Like what?" Yokes asked, her voice formal.

"Never mind," Harry replied. Officer Yokes was on the job, after all. "Look, aren't you curious about why Gertie disappeared five years ago? Haven't you asked yourself where she went? What she did? How she survived?"

"It's not my case," Yokes began, turning to face her in the hallway. She looked troubled.

"But how can Calvin close this case without knowing?" Harry asked. "I find that incredible."

"We know how she died —" Yokes said.

Harry just stared at her.

"The physical evidence —"

"Isn't everything," Harry said firmly.

Yokes stared back. She had nice eyes, Harry noted absently.

"There's no evidence that a crime was committed," Yokes replied. "People disappear all the time, and a lot of them don't want to be found."

"A terminally ill woman who needed constant medical care?" Harry scoffed.

"It's not unheard of," Yokes answered. "You'd be surprised."

"Maybe I would," Harry admitted. "But it just doesn't make any sense."

"Calvin is a good detective. If he thinks that the case is closed, then the case is closed," Yokes retorted. She turned and walked down the hall to the stairs, leaving Harry no choice but to follow her. "Just go down those steps and take a left."

"Thanks."

"Don't mention it," Yokes replied. "I'll give you a call when your statement is typed."

"Hey, I don't even know your name," Harry said, hesitating on the top step.

"Kathleen. Kate," Yokes said over her shoulder. "Now go find your friend and eat something you like."

"Yeah, right," Harry said. She glanced at her watch and then ran down the steps; it was way past noon, and even though that vile tuna sandwich had ruined her appetite, she was going to order the biggest lunch of her life. She had to do something to get the horrible taste of tuna out of her mouth. And the taste of the benign neglect of cops who, in the end, didn't give a damn about a dead old woman.

I can't imagine a police officer grilling someone who was just an innocent bystander. You should make a complaint," Judy said indignantly.

"I guess he was just doing his job. Trying to find out what I knew," Harry said, looking down at her plate. There was still food on it, but she was too troubled to finish it. Judy had been acting strangely ever since she had found her waiting on the ground floor of the police station, although Harry couldn't quite put her finger on what was bothersome about her lover's behaviour. Judy had certainly exhibited all the right reactions — concern that Harry had nearly fainted during her interview with Calvin, anger that Calvin would push her hard enough to make her light-headed. But still, something felt wrong. It was as if Judy had to think about what came next instead of responding naturally. Her reactions seemed artificial, her attention wandered, her mood was indeterminate: pensive one moment, frivolous the next. In short, there was something else on her mind.

"Well, I've never been interviewed by the police, so I wouldn't really know. But I still think he was pretty insensitive," Judy said.

Harry shrugged. "The whole thing was quite disconcerting."

"I wish I could have been there with you," Judy said.

"Me too."

"Well, it's over. You don't have to think about it any more," Judy said.

She was right, Harry thought. Except that she couldn't get it out of her mind. And whatever was bothering Judy, it was making her twitchy.

"So what would you like to do now?" Judy asked.

Harry stifled a burp and said, "drive Bug up the coast and escape from this hell-hole."

"How can you say that after such a wonderful meal?" Judy teased.

"Easily," Harry retorted dryly.

"Especially once your hunger's been assuaged," Judy joked.

"Especially," Harry replied. "But even with a full stomach, I feel like I've inadvertently stumbled into another world, one I don't like very much."

"The decor of this restaurant is on the overdone side, but I suppose that's to attract tourists," Judy responded.

Her tone was light but her smile false, which further distressed Harry. "I guess so," she replied, glancing with distaste at the garishly painted walls, the floor with its shiny tiles of over-bright primary colours and the orange fishnets which hung from the ceiling like a large, floating sculpture conjured up by a giant spider.

Judy rapped her knuckles on the vermilion formica tabletop, and said, "What's this, some kind of plastic? There's probably not a genuine piece of wood in the whole place. The food was certainly good, though. And your crab patties looked scrumptious. I'm surprised you didn't finish them."

"That wretched tuna sandwich ruined my appetite," Harry replied.

"How barbaric!" Judy exclaimed with a contrived shudder. "Now that's certainly something to complain about."

Harry smiled.

"No, really," Judy said brightly.

"Actually, when I said I didn't much like things here, I wasn't referring to the rather tacky decor, or to the food," Harry said, tiring of whatever game they were playing, tacit or not. "I was referring to what happened to Gertrude Cashin."

"But the police are satisfied that she killed herself, aren't they?" Judy asked.

Harry finished her second cup of decaffeinated coffee and looked around the restaurant. It was filled despite the mid-afternoon hour. "Yes. And I believe them. But it's strange that they aren't curious about where she was for the past five years."

"And you are."

Harry nodded.

"Harry, do you think you should be getting involved in this?" Judy asked. "You don't know anything about Gertrude Cashin. What if she was involved in something illegal?"

"That's absurd! She was seriously ill, fighting to stay alive. Besides, the police would have said something," Harry retorted, watching a nuclear family consisting of mom, pop and two half-grown kids, one of each sex, silently and methodically eat their way through platter-sized servings of steak, ribs and ketchup-drenched fries. She averted her eyes, not particularly wanting to add a bout of gay angst to the confusion she was already experiencing.

"Not necessarily," Judy replied. "Once she was dead, there would be no point in the police investigating further. Perhaps you should leave it be."

"What, are you related to Johnnie Calvin?" Harry replied bitterly. Didn't anyone care about Gertie? But perhaps she was being unrealistic; after all, why should the cops give a damn? And why should Judy? She had never met her.

"Harry, I'm just being logical. You spent what, less than an hour with the woman? Be sensible!" Judy hissed impatiently, carelessly tossing her napkin on the table. Harry wondered whether she was going to finish her salmon filet, contemplated offering to do it for her, then swiftly abandoned the idea. Indigestion was already looming, and not from the food, which had been tasty, if over-abundant.

"It just doesn't seem right," Harry said stubbornly. Although she had inadvertently stumbled into this mess, she found it difficult to contemplate walking away from it when there were so many unanswered questions. Especially when everything was so fresh in her mind. She had repeated her story twice for Calvin, and later today she was going to have to read, verify and then sign a police statement which reiterated everything in black and white, a statement which was probably being plunked out letter by letter by the most delectable policewoman Harry had ever met. Not that she was in the habit of making the acquaintance of policewomen, either recreationally or in the line of duty, but still. She could envision the attractive Kate Yokes sweating over some ancient police station typewriter which had crooked letters and a worn out ribbon to produce an accurate rendition of her precious words. But she was probably romanticizing the whole procedure; Kate Yokes was likely sitting in front of a computer screen, keyboarding sixty words a minute. At that rate, she would finish Harry's report in half an hour.

"You feel guilty, don't you?" Judy said with a sigh.

"Not really," Harry lied. "But Gertrude Cashin was an interesting old woman. She was really sick, although I didn't know that then.

If I had, I would have spent more time with her. She gave me a towel to dry my hair because I was soaked from the storm. She invited me, a total stranger, into her apartment, made me coffee, gave me brandy to drink. We talked. She told me she was a lesbian. Then I left, and she committed suicide."

"I didn't know she was a lesbian," Judy said. "But Harry, I don't see how that changes things. You didn't *know* her. You just happened to be there that night."

"But don't you see, nobody cares!" Harry exclaimed in frustration.

"Shhh — people are staring," Judy whispered, reaching out to pat Harry's hand.

Feeling patronized, Harry yanked it away and ignored Judy's hurt look, although she lowered her voice. "I don't care. It's the truth."

"Maybe it is, maybe it isn't. There might be a lot of people who are grieving right at this very moment. You don't know if she had family, friends, lovers. But even if she didn't, it's not your responsibility," Judy said.

"You think I should just forget about it, don't you?"

Judy lowered her eyes and sighed. "I don't know, Harry, I really don't. I just don't want you to be obsessed with it."

Harry slumped in her chair, then fiddled with her empty coffee cup. "Let's go back to the motel."

"I'm not finished eating yet," Judy replied calmly, without looking up from her lunch. Harry could see that the sauce on her salmon had cooled and congealed, but Judy separated a piece of fish and forked it into her mouth.

"It must be cold," Harry commented. "Why don't you ask them to re-heat it?"

Another fork-full made its way to Judy's mouth. Harry watched Judy's fork rise and fall as it whittled away at the piece of salmon on her plate, the rhythmic, silent motion of her jaw as she chewed, the withdrawn expression in her eyes.

"Look, this just won't do," Harry blurted. It was all too reminiscent of their chocolate croissant and coffee brunch in Provincetown, when, for the first time in their relationship, they had been unable to communicate across the width of a restaurant table. They couldn't continue to bicker like this, sniping at each other as if they were enemies under the skin, strangers despite fervent professions of love. She was sure now that something was wrong, very wrong, but she didn't know what it was.

Judy placed her fork next to the knife on her plate and grimaced. "I know."

"And you're right, of course," Harry said swiftly. "I didn't know Gertrude Cashin, and I have no good reason to get involved. It's clear that she killed herself to escape a brutally painful death from cancer. It seems like an open and shut case, except for the fact that she disappeared for five years. But still, I want to know what happened to her," Harry confessed. "I can't deny that it sounds crazy —"

"Not crazy," Judy interrupted. "Stupid, maybe, but not crazy."

"Thanks," Harry said wryly. "But imagine how you'd feel if you'd met someone who killed themselves shortly after. And then imagine that that person had been missing for the past five years. Wouldn't you want to know where they'd been?"

"Not necessarily," Judy replied.

"Oh, come on," Harry scoffed.

"All right. Naturally, I'd be curious, just like anyone else," Judy admitted, fiddling with her fork until it was perfectly aligned with the knife. Both utensils sank slowly into the thick, pink sauce. Harry thought it looked disgusting. "But if the police aren't interested, why should you be?"

Judy was right, of course. But only to a point. She hadn't been there. She hadn't met Gertie. She hadn't dreamed of Gertie. "Because I need to know," Harry said slowly. "Maybe I could have forgotten if we had stayed in Provincetown. Maybe it wouldn't have seemed so real once I was away from the Seashore Motel and this damn town with its fog and rain. But then we came back here so I could talk to the police. I don't know why, Judy, but I *feel* involved."

"Harry, we should go to the motel and see if your policewoman has left a message," Judy said firmly. "If she has, then you can run down and sign it, and this will be over with once and for all."

On the surface of things, yes; but not in her mind, Harry thought.

"Can't you see that what you're proposing is ludicrous? What are you planning to do, go around questioning people and poking your nose into their private affairs? Are you going to ask each and every citizen of this town whether he or she kidnapped Gertrude Cashin? Or helped her disappear? Or ran off with her for some reason known only to themselves?" Judy asked.

It did sound silly when Judy stated it in such bald terms, but it would take more than that to derail her. So what if she had no experience as a detective other than getting to the bottom of her students' disputes by determining which distraught girl's accusations were more exaggerated? She could tell the difference between convolution and complexity, between lies and forgetfulness, between being misled and being confused. She knew how to ask questions, to solve the minor and often petty mysteries which arose at school, and how was this any different? Certainly it was far more serious, but she was intelligent, she was curious, and people liked her. They would open up and tell her what she wanted to know. "I'll manage," Harry said.

"Well, don't expect me to help," Judy said.

"I won't," Harry replied, feeling depressed. "Let's go."

They paid the bill and left the restaurant.

Bug lit the way through the swirling fog. Harry sat in the passenger seat, arms crossed, knees together, chilled to the bone. She stared out the front windshield, although the fog was so thick that there was nothing to see. A stray leaf slapped the glass just below her line of vision, making her start.

"Almost there," Judy murmured, and Harry felt her hand reassuringly squeeze her shoulder.

It was late afternoon, hours before true darkness would fall, but fog shrouded what light there was and the street lamps had automatically switched on. They gleamed weakly through the mist, barely outlining the driveway to the motel.

"This is it," Harry said.

"I know," said Judy. She veered sharply and steered Bug up the rutted pavement. "Let's see if there's a message," she suggested, holding open the door to the office.

There wasn't.

"Have you got the keys?" Judy asked.

Her face had grown pale, Harry noted, although that could have been a trick of the fog.

"Darn! It's like a sauna in here," Judy complained, switching on the overhead light.

"The maid must have turned off the air conditioner," Harry commented, walking over to the air-conditioning unit beneath the window. She moved the setting to high and switched it on, crinkling her nose when stale air smelling of mildew blasted from the ancient and obviously dirty machine.

"Harry, I want to talk to you," Judy said, pulling out the chair from the desk and sitting down.

This was it, Harry thought as she perched on the edge of the bed. Now she was going to find out what was bothering Judy.

"I know this is bad timing —"

"Oh god, you're going to leave me," Harry muttered, covering her mouth with a hand.

"Will you stop being so insecure? Every time we have a fight, you think that I'm going to leave you," Judy gently berated her.

"Sorry."

"I'm not breaking up with you. I just want to be by myself for a little while," Judy said.

There was a difference?

"And no, I'm not going to see Lorna, if that's what you're thinking," she added.

Harry didn't want to admit that she was so stunned she had been unable to think. Yet. "But why?"

"I'm not sure I can explain it to you."

"Try."

"It's mainly because I'm confused," Judy said with a lopsided smile.

Harry ignored it. She didn't want smiles, platitudes or cliches, she wanted genuine answers. "About Lorna? About us? What?"

"About myself. I'm going to turn fifty this year, and I'm increasingly unclear about who I am and what I want to do with the rest of my life," Judy said. "Oh, I know I want to spend it with you, but, as important as you are to me, there are other things I'm not pleased with."

"Like what?"

"My relationships with other people, for one thing. Even with you," Judy said.

"Why didn't you tell me?" Harry asked. And what was wrong with their relationship? What had she done? Or forgotten to do?

"There wasn't anything to tell," Judy said. "It sort of built up gradually. I was feeling discontented, although there wasn't any one thing I could put my finger on. But once I was down here and had time to think, I realized that I had to do something about it. I'm just sorry that I let myself become involved with Lorna, and that my indiscretion is going to make this more threatening to you than it should be."

Lorna or not, Harry had never felt so dismayed. "You said you weren't dissatisfied with our relationship —"

"It's not you Harry, it's me," Judy interrupted.

Harry didn't understand. "Haven't I —"

"You've been everything I ever wanted," Judy said. "That's not the problem."

Then what was, Harry wondered.

"I simply don't want to feel dissatisfied at the end of my life," Judy said vehemently.

Harry was shocked into silence.

"I want to live my life to the fullest, and I have to be clear on the best way to do it," Judy added. "It's not enough to get up in the morning, go to work, come home and sit in front of the television every night."

"But we don't watch TV every night," Harry protested.

"You know what I mean," Judy said impatiently. "Watch TV, read a book, play cards, go out to the bar — it's all the same after a while. I feel like my life is stale, stagnant. People come, people go, and it doesn't seem to make any difference."

"We have some good friends," Harry reminded her.

"With whom we always go to the same places and talk about the same things," Judy pointed out. "Don't you ever wish that something, anything, would change?"

"No," Harry replied. She had thought that that was what life was all about. You found a woman to love, and you built a home with her. You accumulated a few possessions, nice ones, gathered a few friends, good ones, and took pleasure from simple things. Reading a well-written book, for example. Or taking in a thought-provoking movie. Softball and picnics and weekends at a rented cottage in the summer, line dancing and skiing in the winter. Making love with the same woman, cherishing the familiarity. She had also believed that everyone craved security, and depended on the people around them to provide it by being reliable, trustworthy, honest. When had Judy started struggling with the central premise of their life together? Perhaps her affair with Lorna had been an indication of things to come rather than an event provoked by exceptional circumstances. Perhaps Judy wanted to take more risks. Perhaps she needed other lovers. Was this the direction she was going, with Harry's resistance the main impediment she had to overcome? Harry gulped. "How long have you been feeling like this?"

"Long enough to want to do something about it before it's too late," Judy said.

"Can't we work through it together?" Harry said desperately.

"No," Judy said with a shake of her head.

"I don't understand," Harry whispered, more to herself than to Judy.

"Oh, Harry, please realize that I'm not trying to hurt you. But this is something I have to do for myself," Judy said. "Please don't be so upset."

Harry remained silent.

"I thought it might be too much to expect," Judy said sadly.

Harry looked up at Judy. "What do you want me to say?"

"That after having lived with me for ten years, that after all those years of sharing our innermost thoughts and fears, you can deal with it. That you will make the effort to understand, to grant me this gift, this time for myself. That you trust me enough to know that I wouldn't jeopardize our relationship for anything," Judy replied, moving to the bed and sitting down beside Harry.

"I do trust you," Harry said softly, throwing caution to the wind, especially when, down deep, she knew that she didn't. Not enough to believe that a rejuvenated Judy would still feel the same about her. "I really do."

Judy kissed her, a gentle kiss of gratitude which blossomed swiftly into passion and made Harry's knees weak. "I'd better go," Judy said, disengaging Harry's hands and rising from the bed.

"Now? Tonight?" Harry protested, panic-stricken.

"I think I should leave right away," Judy said, her voice kind. "It's not going to do either of us any good to draw this out."

"But your things —" Harry protested.

"I can come back and get them later," Judy interrupted as she walked to the door.

Oh, god. Her nightmares had come true. Gertie had been right, only it hadn't been Lorna, who, it seemed, was inconsequential when it came right down to it. For what was a momentary fling with an old lover when Judy was looking for the perfection? Come to think of it, what was she?

"Harry, it's going to be all right. You'll see," Judy reassured her.

Harry sat on the bed and watched the door close behind her lover and then fell back on the rough bedspread and had a good cry.

Is Kathleen Yokes there?" Harry asked, running fingers through her hair, which was still damp from her shower.

"No, I think she's already left," replied a youthful male voice at the other end of the line. Harry could hear the constant hum of the police station behind him, like a hive of bees in blue swarming to uphold law and order.

"Are you sure?" Harry persisted. She couldn't believe that Kate had gone off duty without finishing typing up her statement and calling her to come in and sign it.

"Yeah," the voice confirmed impatiently. "I saw her go out the front door," he added.

"Oh."

"Do you want to leave a message?" he inquired tiredly.

"I guess so," Harry replied, although she wasn't sure what to say. "Get your butt over here right this minute" would appear overly aggressive, while "please don't make me spend another night in this miserable place" would sound like a plea for deliverance. Which wouldn't be far off the mark.

"Miss?"

"Just tell her I called to see when my statement will be ready for me to sign," Harry sighed, giving her name and the telephone number of the motel.

"Sure," he said. He sounded bored, and Harry wondered if he was writing anything down. "Oh, wait. She's just come back in." There was a crash, as if he had dropped the telephone on the desk, and then Kate Yokes came on the line.

"Ms. Hubbley?"

"Yes. Is my statement ready, Officer Yokes?" Harry asked.

"It's nearly finished, Ms. Hubbley. Nearly finished," Kate said.

"Will I be able to sign it tonight?" Harry asked.

"I was thinking more like tomorrow morning," Kate replied hopefully.

Harry pressured her with silence.

"Well, I guess I could finish it tonight. I've just got a little over a page to transcribe," Kate replied with a noticeable lack of enthusiasm. "Will you be at your motel in half an hour?"

"Yes," Harry responded.

"I'll drop by with it, then," Kate told her.

"Great," Harry said. "See you later."

It was better than nothing, Harry thought as she hung up the telephone. Kathleen Yokes must be a conscientious policewoman, especially if she was willing to work late to finish something she could just as easily leave for tomorrow. Either that or she had been as aware of Harry as Harry had been of her during that trying interview with Detective John Calvin. Harry snorted; of course Kate Yokes had been *aware* of her — it had been her job to write down every single word Harry had uttered. She shouldn't try to make nothing into something simply because Kate Yokes was a lesbian. Attraction was one thing, desperation quite another. With that depressing thought, she decided it was time to stop feeling sorry for herself, to do something, anything. She dressed in casual slacks and a sweatshirt and went into the bathroom to comb her cowlick into submission. That having taken five whole minutes, she switched on the television and sat down in front of it to watch the news while she waited, trying not to think about Judy.

That, of course, was an impossibility. She wondered where Judy was having dinner and what she had ordered, whether she was drinking beer or wine or mineral water, and succeeded in making herself hungry. And thirsty. She got up and had a drink of water. Then it occurred to her that Judy might be too upset to have dinner. She could have gone straight to her motel room, since, after all, she must be staying somewhere, unless she was planning to take a bus, train or plane back to Montreal late tonight or to rent a car, park on a deserted street and sleep in the back seat, although this was definitely not a Judy-like thing to do. These days, though, who knew?

Why couldn't she conquer her anxiety?

Shush. Be quiet. Dampen the paranoia. Judy was not a manipulator. They loved each other, and they would find common ground again. Judy shot straight from the hip, hated lingering conflict, and believed that relationships should work. She wanted to go back to Montreal with a an unmuddied palate, a plan for the future.

Her future.

No, their future.

Harry squirmed in her chair, annoyed by the bleating of the television. She would read until Kate Yokes arrived. She picked up her book and settled on the bed just as there was a firm rap on the door.

"Yes?"

"It's Kate Yokes," came the reply.

Harry got up from the bed and opened the door. "Come in."

"Here's your statement," Kate said with a smile as Harry closed the door. She was no longer in uniform, but Harry still found the policewoman attractive. There was an unusual authority in the way she moved, as if she knew her body well and was comfortable with it. The tailored suit she was wearing didn't hurt, either.

"Great," Harry responded, taking the sheaf of papers from her. "It won't take me long to read it, and then you can get on with your evening."

"Actually, I was wondering if you had eaten yet," Kate said. "If not, perhaps we could have dinner together."

Harry stopped reading and looked at her, more startled by the warmth in her eyes than by the invitation to dinner. There had been safety in speculating from a distance, but she didn't feel so safe any more.

"I was about to leave for the night and pick up something at one of the take-out places when you called," Kate explained. "Since you sounded like it was urgent, I put dinner off until I finished typing your statement, and frankly, I'm starved."

Harry glanced at the travel alarm sitting on the bedside table. It was nearly seven-thirty, her stomach was growling, and she was alone. "Well, why not?" she replied, more to herself than to Kate. Having dinner with a good-looking woman was infinitely more interesting than sitting in a musty-smelling motel room, waiting for Judy to drop by to pick up her clothes only to leave again. Better to admit that she couldn't think her way through this, at least not yet. She would drink some dry white wine, eat a little seafood and engage in scintillating conversation. If she could ever stop thinking about Judy.

"Any preferences?" Kate asked.

"What?" Harry said rather distractedly, tossing her keys into her purse.

"Any type of food you prefer?" Kate paraphrased, opening the door.

"No."

Each waited for the other to walk through the doorway, and then their eyes met. Kate's were bright with suppressed amusement and something else, something dangerous enough that Harry left it unnamed. It was just dinner, she reassured herself. They weren't going on a date, for pete's sake, so why should she worry? She was a big girl now, and a little snap, crackle and pop over dinner was something which she could handle. And enjoy. Who wouldn't? And who would blame her? After what she'd been through in the past few days, innocently chatting with a woman who was going to kill herself later that evening and hadn't been courteous enough to tell her, discovering that her lover had problems that she, Harry, couldn't solve, needs which she, Harry, couldn't meet, well, after all that, didn't she deserve some fun, a little distraction in her life?

"Let me put it another way, then. Is there anything you absolutely detest?"

They relinquished chivalry simultaneously and bumped into each other in the narrow doorway.

"No," Harry replied with a breathless laugh.

"I feel like I'm having a goddamn identity crisis," Kate snorted.

"Never mind," Harry replied with amusement, pulling the door shut behind her.

"My car or yours?" Kate asked.

"It doesn't matter," Harry responded.

"Let's take mine, then," Kate suggested, pointing across the street to an ancient red convertible, its top down in spite of the damp air and ever-present fog. At least it had temporarily stopped raining.

"I'm impressed," Harry admitted.

"That's why I bought it," Kate retorted.

"Now why did I know that?" Harry said, smothering a laugh. How predictable. How refreshing in a perversely trite way. Still, it worked.

Harry watched Kate jump over the door and land smack in the middle of the driver's seat without impaling herself on the steering wheel or the gear shift. She measured the distance from the sidewalk to the top of the door on the passenger side, tried a little experimental hop, then gave up and opened the door and slid in. It was Kate's car, after all, so let her play the perfect butch. Not that she was bad at it, Harry admitted to herself. Not at all. She was probably just showing off. She and Judy joked about Judy's femme tendencies and Harry's butch ones, but roles weren't *that* in these days. Harry knew she was more inclined to take the lead in lovemaking, but assertion between the sheets did not a butch make. After all, Judy liked to drive more than she did, and wasn't that supposed to be a butch thing too?

Talk about butches behind the wheel, Harry thought wryly. She had barely fastened her seatbelt when the car roared into the street. Kate drove like a cop chasing a murderer, and Harry wondered whether she had taken part in high-speed chases or if she was just showing off. The convertible attacked the slick pavement like a rabid dog off the leash, barely slowing down to take the corners. Harry sat ramrod straight and resisted the urge to hold on.

"Here we are," Kate announced, deftly parking the convertible in an improbably tiny spot between two cars without nudging either of them.

"Where's the restaurant, down the street somewhere?" Harry asked, ignoring Kate as she once again jumped over the closed door. "Oh, I thought we'd just order out," Kate replied, leading the way up a gravel walk. Harry watched her pull her keys from her pocket and open two professional-looking locks. "Welcome to my humble abode," she said, ushering Harry in and switching on the light. "There isn't much room. It's only a one-and-a-half, but then again, I'm not home much, anyway."

"Uh-huh," Harry replied, looking around. It was small but cosy in a claustrophobic sort of way. Kate's single bed was by far the largest piece of furniture in the room. A half-size refrigerator was sitting on one side of the sink, a small microwave oven on the other. The walls were painted off-white, almost the same colour as Kate's suit, and there were framed prints on the walls, most of them of semi-naked women posed in pastel surroundings. They were as stylized as air-blown photographs. Harry had seen prints like these in the living rooms of half the lesbians she knew. The full nudes were reserved for bedrooms, or, occasionally, the bathroom.

"This way you'll have some peace and quiet to go over your report," Kate said. "Here, have a seat," she added, motioning to a wood chair which she pulled from the corner and placed facing the bed.

Harry sat down.

Kate opened a TV-table and slid it in front of Harry. Surprisingly, the design was of huge, drooping flowers. Harry had expected horses, cars or guns. Something suitably macho. Maybe the TV-tables had been a gift from a former lover, or, more likely, from a relative who knew less about Kathleen Yokes than he or she realized.

"Why don't you get that over with and then I'll order out?" Kate suggested.

Harry took the typed statement from her purse and placed it on the table in front of her. She began to read her statement, wincing at how insipid it sounded. Spoken words float away like petals in a stream; they might sound significant when uttered, but their transience makes them forgivable. The listener reads intent, measures importance, responds immediately. Later the utterer can pretend that she was misinterpreted, that the listener emphasized the wrong word, that her memory was faulty. Not so with the written word. Its permanence made it a weapon which could be used to ridicule, to shame, to convict, if not of guilt, of oversight, or, conversely, exaggeration or falsity.

Harry turned the page and kept reading. She could hear Kate bustling in the background, the sound of plates being removed from the shelf, the metallic clatter of cutlery being withdrawn from a drawer.

"Beer or wine?"

"Wine would be fine," Harry replied.

"Red or white?"

"White."

Harry read on, remembering how she had driven up the driveway to a nearly deserted motel, despite the fact that its sign wasn't lit. Her allergy to dust. Gertie handing her a towel. Drying her dripping hair. The dirt streaks on the towel. Gertie turning the registration book around so Harry could sign it. Gertie asking her back to her apartment, which wasn't dusty. Sitting down in a chair and having a drink with a woman who was soon going to die. The things she had said, Gertie's replies. She skimmed the rest, verifying that nothing had been omitted, altered or misunderstood, and then turned over the stapled sheaf of papers so that she didn't have to look at it any more.

"Something wrong?" Kate asked, handing Harry a glass of wine. "Did I make a mistake? Leave something out?"

"No," Harry replied, sipping the wine, pleased to discover that it was a dry chablis which had been perfectly chilled. She took another sip.

Kate opened the other TV-table, sat down on the bed, and placed the table in front of her. "Not exactly the ideal dining room table, but it does the job," she said.

Harry nodded and sipped her wine. "Do I sign at the end, or what?"

"Yes. And then initial every page, and I'll do the same," Kate replied, getting up and moving behind Harry.

Harry signed her name on the last page, conscious of Kate standing over her, aware of her closeness. She could smell the cleanness of her clothes, and there were hints of the herbal shampoo she must have used that morning ... or perhaps more recently, if she had prepared for this ... But she couldn't have. Or could she? Harry's fingers tightened around the base of the pen as she swiftly scribbled her initials on the bottom of each page. "Done," she announced brusquely, still leaning over the TV-table, wishing she could move further away and put some distance between herself and Kate Yokes, who, even standing still, was sending strong enough signals to wake a dyke in a deep coma. And Harry certainly wasn't comatose, not one little bit. Just the opposite.

"Good," Kate said in a husky voice.

"Yes, I'm thankful that's over," Harry admitted.

Kate leaned over and took her statement. "I'll sign it later."

Harry felt Kate's fingers stroke the nape of her neck. "I hate mixing business with pleasure," Kate whispered with a brief laugh.

"But you're a policewoman," Harry said in half-hearted protest.

"And you're not wanted for anything. At least not for committing a crime," Kate replied with a tight laugh.

Harry's nerve endings screamed with pleasure. "I don't think I can —"

"Our professional relationship ended when you signed on the dotted line," Kate said lightly, her fingers continuing their voyage up and down Harry's neck. "Your problem is that you think too much. This is better," she said, and then she was bending to kiss Harry.

Harry wasn't sure, but she let herself be led, waiting passively for a response to develop.

Kate lifted Harry's sweatshirt. "I love how you look in a bra," she breathed, staring at Harry's body.

"Madonna the second," Harry joked, feeling uncomfortable.

"Better than Madonna," Kate said seriously, looking into Harry's eyes for a second and then burying her face between Harry's breasts. Harry felt her fingers stroke her through her bra, at first gently and then more urgently. Kate's tongue wet her cleavage, and then slid under the cloth of her bra, searching.

"I can't, Kate," Harry whispered.

Kate released her at once and moved to sit on the bed.

"I'm sorry," Harry said humbly, pulling down her sweatshirt.

"Bad timing," Kate mumbled.

"Yes," Harry agreed. "Yes, it is bad timing. My lover told me tonight that she needed to go away for a while to sort things out, which was a hell of a shock. I'm attracted to you, but I just can't concentrate."

"I've wanted you since I saw you in the police station," Kate said. "And I thought the feeling was mutual."

"I was attracted to you," Harry said gently. "And I still am. But doing something about it is new for me. I've been with Judy for ten years, and I've never been involved with anyone else in all that time."

"I suppose I should feel complimented," Kate said, "but I don't."

"I should go," Harry said gently, feeling guilty as hell.

"No, please stay," Kate replied swiftly. "We can watch television, or talk, or maybe even get drunk," she added with a cynical laugh. "Or not."

"I'm afraid I wouldn't be very good company," Harry confessed. "I think I need to be alone."

Kate nodded reluctantly. "I'll drive you."

"No, I'll take a cab," Harry responded.

Kate looked relieved. Harry watched her walk across the room, pick up the telephone receiver and order a taxi.

"I can wait outside if you like," she offered.

"Don't be silly," Kate said with a shaky laugh. "It's not your fault. And it's not the end of the world."

"I suppose not," Harry said. Sometimes the desire was present but the timing off. Other times opportunity was there, but not the desire. When it worked it was magical, when it didn't, it could be messy.

"I'm a bit upset myself these days," Kate said, pouring herself another glass of wine.

"What about?" Harry asked, turning away from the window and letting the curtains fall shut.

"Oh, you know, things," Kate said vaguely, avoiding Harry's eyes.

"What things?" Harry persisted.

Kate sighed. "My lover Lila and I just agreed to separate."

"That's horrible," Harry exclaimed. "What happened?"

"Oh, the usual," Kate shrugged. "She's a doctor. I met her after she graduated from medical school and set up private practice in Hyannis Port. We were both seeing other women at the time, but we started dating later on, and eventually we moved in together. But it's not as easy as you think to make a go of it in private practice, and the pressure was really intense. A couple of years ago she was offered a staff job at a hospital in Boston, so she sold her practice and moved. After that, we could only be together the rare times when both of us weren't working. Sometimes I'd drive up and stay with her, sometimes she'd drive down and stay here. But it was hard to have a long-distance relationship, and lonely, too. She wanted to see other women, I didn't. We argued about it. She never said so, but I'm sure she started dating. I guess I shouldn't have been surprised."

"You must be really upset," Harry responded, trying not to compare Kate's situation to her own. She heard a car drive down the street and turned back toward the window. "When did this happen?"

"A couple of weeks ago."

"How long were you together?"

"Nearly nine years," Kate said despondently. "You know, what hurts the most is that we didn't break up because we didn't love each other any more, we broke up because we couldn't agree on how we wanted to live together. We couldn't agree on the fundamentals. I still love her very much, but I have to get on with my life."

Harry sighed and slumped against the wall. Comparisons were patently unavoidable.

"I applied for a job with the Boston Police Department; my name is probably still on the waiting list. Should I have given up my career for her?" Kate asked. "Or her for me?"

The question was of necessity rhetorical, so Harry didn't answer it.

"It's tough when you realize you don't love somebody enough," Kate said.

"God, yes!" Harry said fervently, thinking of Gertie's lover Vera. And of Judy.

"Gertrude Cashin was my lover's aunt," Kate added.

"What?"

"So that's been upsetting me too," Kate continued, oblivious to Harry's astonishment. "When you're a cop, you try to put all that personal shit out of your mind so it doesn't interfere with your work, but it's been hard."

"You knew her?"

"Sure. Quite well. My lover was close to her aunt, and I adored her. She was such a grand old lady, such a dyke. We used to get together on a regular basis and talk about how it was in the old days. She could tell some fascinating stories about the Cape. Boston, too. We often had dinner with her, or just went over to visit for a couple of hours," Kate said. "During the week, when I was working night shift and Lila was busy during the day, I'd often drop by alone. She was good company."

"And then she disappeared," Harry said, recalling Kate's comments during and after her interview at the police station. Kate had acted as if Gertie's disappearance didn't mean a thing. Why?

"Yes," Kate replied, emptying her glass.

"Didn't you think that was strange?" Harry asked.

"Of course. What do you think?" Kate replied. "She was a friend, a close friend."

"But didn't you do anything about it?" Harry persisted.

"Like what?" Kate said, looking uncomfortable.

"You work for the police," Harry said, glancing out the window. A cab was parked outside the apartment. Damn. She was going to have to leave, and there were so many questions she wanted to ask. "Surely there must have been something you could have done."

"You saw the kind of jobs they give me," Kate said with a bitter laugh. "I get to take dictation, type up reports, direct traffic at funerals. Sometimes they even remember that I've been through the same training they have, and let me patrol the streets at night."

"But Kate, she was ill. Seriously ill. Didn't you worry about her?" Harry pressed as the taxi driver honked twice.

"Of course I was worried about her!" Kate exclaimed, sounding agitated. Harry watched her fill her wine glass. Her hands were shaking. "And so was Lila. As a doctor, she understood better than I did how much work it took to keep Gertie alive and out of pain. Look, the department did all the right things. But you don't realize how many people get reported missing in this country. They just go off one day and never come back. Or they come back when they damn well feel like it. The majority of missing persons are missing because they want to be, which doesn't make police forces very motivated when it comes to tracking them down. Especially when so many of them tell you to go to hell once you do find them. So you can't blame the police if they prefer to concentrate on solving real crimes."

"Do you mean to tell me that you think Gertie vanished of her own free will?" Harry said disbelievingly.

"I don't know," Kate sighed. "But there was no evidence of coercion."

"But where would she go? And why? How could she have managed to live in hiding for five years?" Harry asked, waving her hand through the window at the taxi driver in an attempt to calm him down. It did no good; the horn continued to blare.

"Don't you think I've asked myself those questions a million times?" Kate asserted. "Just because I'm a cop doesn't mean I have any more answers than you do."

The driver leaned on the horn. "Kate —"

"You'd better go before he has a stroke."

"But —"

"I really don't want to talk about it any more," Kate said abruptly.

"But who looked after the motel while she was gone?" Harry asked, certain that Kate knew.

"I said I didn't want to talk about it," Kate responded forcefully. "Not right now."

"Fine," Harry said brusquely. She was frustrated, but there was no point in being persistent, not while Kate's feathers were ruffled. She was going to have to find a way to ask questions about Gertie's disappearance without seeming to criticize Kate's performance as a policewoman.

"It's too upsetting," Kate added.

"I understand," Harry replied, although she suspected that in part, Kate was hiding behind her distress. Then she felt vile for doubting her sincerity. "Can I call you?" she asked Kate.

Kate nodded, kissed her lightly on the cheek without making eye contact, and shooed her out the door.

The taxi driver gave her royal hell all the way back to the motel and left her in such a wretched mood that she didn't give him a tip. She heard him curse as he counted the cash she handed him, but she didn't look back as he gunned the engine and roared from the parking lot. It was his life he was shortening, not hers, she thought as she ran into the office and eagerly asked if there were any messages. Surely Judy would have called by now.

"Nothing for you, Miss Hubbley," the manager said.

Damn, damn, and double-damn, Harry grumbled as she hurried to her room, giving Bug a good-night pat on her way by. She slumped in the chair and looked at her watch. It was too early for bed, too late to take in a movie. There was nothing to do but read her book or watch television, and she knew that neither would hold her attention, not when she was waiting for Judy to call, to walk in and hug her and say that everything was all right.

Oh, grow up, she told herself viciously. Judy was doing what she had to do. And there was something she could do, something she had told Judy she was going to do, and that was to investigate Gertrude Cashin's disappearance and death.

What a bombshell Kate had unloaded! Harry never would have guessed that Kate had been a close friend of Gertie's from the way Kate had downplayed the mystery surrounding Gertie's disappearance. The problem was, what did this mean, if anything? Gertie had committed suicide because she was terminally ill and in excruciating pain. There was no evidence to the contrary, and no one suspected foul play.

Still, it was disconcerting that at the police station this morning, Kate hadn't admitted that she had been a friend of Gertie's. But perhaps this wasn't as mysterious it appeared to be. Perhaps Kate had assumed that everyone knew about her friendship with Gertie. This was a small town, and people were bound to know each other. It would be strange if they didn't. But Harry wasn't from West Yarmouth, so why would Kate assume she knew?

Why hadn't Kate done more to investigate Gertie's disappearance? Hadn't she been perplexed about why someone with incurable cancer would choose to vanish? And if she and Gertie were close friends, wasn't it conceivable that Gertie had dropped a few hints about her intentions? And what about Lila? Wouldn't Gertie be tempted to mention something about her plans to her niece?

Harry sighed and got up and peered out the window. The fog had drifted out to sea again, and the cars on the road were visible, as was the light in the window of the Seashore Motel office. It wasn't possible, she thought, startled. She pressed her nose against the window and squinted. Yes, there was a light; if was flickering sporadically, but it was definitely in the office.

That shouldn't be, she thought worriedly. Not unless the police had come back, and if everything had unfolded as they claimed it had, they had no reason to return. So who was in the Seashore Motel? The case was closed, wasn't it? Or was it? She grabbed her keys, stuffed them into her purse and went out, jogging across the lawn to the edge of the road. The light in the office was more visible from here, but she couldn't see any movement. She waited until there was a break in traffic and ran across the road and up the driveway.

Harry hesitated at the edge of the parking lot, feeling exposed. It was dark, although not impenetrably so, but she grew timid and the hair at the back of her neck rose. If she had been a dog, she probably would have howled.

She forced herself to move, taking the shortest route to the steps to the office, proceeding on tiptoes, which was futile, since anyone in the office could have seen her approach through the picture window and would certainly be waiting for her. What the hell, she decided, bounding up the steps in one mad dash and pounding on the door with wild abandon. She stood stock still, holding her breath and listening, but she couldn't hear a thing. She lifted her hand to knock again, and then realized that the door was ajar. She gave it a gentle push, and it swung inward.

Oh, shit, Harry thought with dismay. Her knees were shaking, but she didn't really believe in ghosts, so she took a tiny step forward and looked into the office. It was empty. And still dusty, she sensed; her nose twitched the moment she moved completely inside. She closed the door and sneezed, and the resulting noise echoed in the empty space.

"Okay, you can come out now," she said in a loud, clear voice. She eased forward, toward the counter.

"Look, it's not funny any more," she shouted, turning around in a complete circle. She was certain someone else was there, but who?

"Please," she urged in a stage whisper. "Please, whoever you are, don't do this to me."

There was no reply. She leaned against the counter and coughed as dust sprayed the air.

"Detective Calvin?"

But she knew that the dour detective wouldn't taunt her like this.

"Kate?"

The silence was pervasive.

"Is it you, Kate?"

Kate wouldn't hide. And if she hadn't wanted to see Harry again tonight, she would have been shrewd enough to escape long before now. Harry wouldn't be an impediment, not to a cop who could jump over car doors without injuring any vital bodily organs.

"Who *are* you?" Harry whimpered.

The door to Gertie's apartment opened and Harry thought she was going to faint. She supported herself on the counter and waited.

"Are you from the police?" came a hesitant voice.

"Who the hell are you?" Harry shouted. "Come out of there so I can see you!"

"It's just me," the person said, moving forward into the light.

Harry stared at him, and recognition suddenly dawned. "Clifford Jones?"

He tilted his head and stared at her.

"Don't you remember? That morning when my car wouldn't start?" Harry asked.

"Oh, right. Yes, I remember," he said with obvious relief. "Sorry, though, but I don't recall your name."

"Harriet Hubbley," Harry replied, and automatically put out her hand.

Clifford shook it.

"Harry," she added.

"Cliff," he said with a nod.

"What are you doing here?" Harry asked, sneezing.

"I couldn't sleep," he replied.

What a lame excuse, Harry thought, sneezing again.

"Are you allergic to dust?" he asked.

Harry nodded.

"Want to come back here?" he asked, gesturing toward the apartment. "At least it's clean."

"That's not such a bad idea," Harry replied, following him through the doorway. "I bet we're not supposed to be here," she said, looking around. She was relieved that everything looked the same. Except that Gertie was dead, and she had died here.

She sat down and watched Cliff lower himself into Gertie's chair.

"You gave me quite a scare," he confessed.

"The feeling is mutual," Harry replied dryly. "But don't worry, I'm not going to report you to the police. I'm staying in the motel across the street, and I wondered why there was a light on in the office, that's all."

"I forgot to turn it off," he mumbled, slapping his forehead. "Dumb, dumb, dumb."

"But why did you come back here in the first place?" she asked.

"I was just looking around," he replied sheepishly.

"Yes, but why?" she persisted, waiting for him to tell her to mind her own business.

"I got to thinking about what had happened, you know, that she was missing for five years, and wondered whether there were any clues the police had missed," he replied.

"Clues?"

"You know, *clues*," he said impatiently. "I'm a pretty impulsive guy, so I decided to drop by tonight."

"That sounds a bit far-fetched," Harry remarked.

He looked so guilty that Harry nearly smiled. He was squirming like a fish impaled on a hook. What on earth could he be hiding?

"There's nothing far-fetched about it," he said officiously. "I'm driving up to Boston in the morning, so this was my last opportunity."

"To check things out," Harry added sceptically. "To look for clues."

"Well, yeah," he replied belligerently.

"So what do you think?"

He stared at her, chewing on his bottom lip. "I don't know what you mean."

"Where do you think Gertie went after she disappeared?" Harry said impatiently. "You're here looking for clues, so you must have something in mind."

"Not really," he replied testily. "And stop treating me like I'm some kind of criminal. I never met the woman before, so how should I know why she wanted to take off?"

"I thought you were interested in finding out, though," Harry said.

"It is sort of mysterious, isn't it?" he asked. "That an old woman would just drop out of sight like that."

"Yes," Harry replied, not giving him any help.

"Well, aren't you curious?" he asked, going on the offensive.

His bottom lip was quivering. What had he been doing before she arrived, Harry wondered? Why did he look so guilty?

"This whole thing has put me behind schedule. I was supposed to be in Boston today, but no, I had to stay and talk to the cops and then wait until my statement was ready to sign. And what could I tell them, anyway? Gertrude Cashin was here when I checked in. I spoke with her. She was a good-looking old lady, obviously sick, but she had a real sense of humour. She had me pegged as a fag seconds after I walked in, although I didn't tell them *that*. The next morning I go to check out and find her dead. The cops tell me that she committed suicide, and that she'd been missing for five years. I don't know anything about that, but it's strange how little they seem to care," Cliff said.

"Quite," Harry agreed.

"So I decided to poke around a bit before I leave for Boston. What's so suspicious about that?"

It was a reasonable question, especially since Harry had intended to do some poking around of her own. But why was he so nervous?

"You know, I wondered whether there was more to it than suicide, and whether the cops were covering up something," he said. "And don't look so shocked. Things like that go on all the time. Once we went back to Canada, who would be around to question what they said? Who would care?"

Kate would care, Harry thought. And her ex-lover Lila. And possibly a long list of other people she and Cliff knew nothing about. "But there seems to be no doubt that she committed suicide," she replied.

"That's what *they* say," he asserted stubbornly.

"But what information would they be hiding? And why?" Harry asked.

"I don't know," he replied. "I'm not a private detective, so I'm at a disadvantage. I don't even know how to go about searching for clues."

"Surely they couldn't conceal the truth. These things don't happen in a vacuum," Harry protested. Still, she didn't know enough about how police departments functioned to even hazard a guess about whether evidence could be hidden, witness statements disappeared, or medical examiner reports falsified. Her knowledge of police procedure was almost nil, gleaned entirely from the few detective shows she had watched on television. "It wouldn't be that easy for a suspicious death to be covered up."

"You're probably right," Cliff said glumly. "Anyway, I'm just going to go home and forget all about it. After all, it's not my problem. And no matter what I do, it won't bring her back. Once you're dead and buried, why or how doesn't really matter very much. Not to the dead person, anyway."

Harry's natural instincts were more of the bulldog type. "I thought you were looking for clues," she said slyly.

"But jeez, I'm just a little ole fag from Toronto," he said with a self-deprecating grin, "and once I got here, I realized I didn't have the faintest idea where to start."

How ingenious, Harry thought sourly. "What did you really come here for, Cliff?"

He looked startled, and for a minute Harry thought he wasn't going to tell her. They he gave a long, audible sigh and reached into his shirt pocket.

"Here," he said, extending his hand. In it was a folded piece of paper.

"What is it?" Harry asked.

"See for yourself," he replied curtly.

Harry gave him an exasperated look, took the sheet of paper from him, and began to unfold it.

"I found it on this table," he said, pointing at the end table next to his chair.

"You what?" Harry exclaimed, suddenly comprehending what she was holding in her hand. She dropped the piece of paper in her lap.

"I didn't mean to take it," he said defensively. "When I couldn't find her, I got worried. I mean, it was obvious that she was very sick, very weak. And then I came in here and saw her body and panicked. I picked up the note and read it, and stuffed it into my pocket without thinking. Then I went back into the office and called the police and went outside to wait for them. I didn't want to stay inside. I couldn't stand being near her body. Once the police arrived, they bustled around, took pictures, and asked a million questions. I just forgot about the note."

An unlikely story, Harry thought, although she couldn't imagine why he would withhold the note from the police. Unless he was lying about not knowing Gertie ... Harry picked up the paper, unfolded it, and read the short, handwritten message.

To my dear friends,

The time has come. All has been resolved. Do not wonder where I was, it is of no consequence now. Do not question what has happened, I have made this decision of my own free will. Do not ponder the involvement of others, for there has been none.

— Gertrude Cashin

"It's a suicide note," she said grimly, looking at him.

"I know," he replied quietly.

"You should have given it to the police," Harry told him.

"Do you think I don't know that?" he replied heatedly. "But imagine how I felt. Being gay, I'm not overly fond of the police at the best of times. You should know how that is," he added, appealing to Harry for sympathy.

She didn't give him any.

"When the police arrived, they were officious as hell," he said. "They weren't particularly friendly, especially Detective Calvin, who took an immediate dislike to me. And I was terribly upset; it isn't every day you discover a corpse, after all. I completely forgot about the note. They questioned me, asked me to come down to the station to make a statement, and then I had to find another place to stay and call the customers I was supposed to meet in Boston. It took time to do all that, especially since I had two sales meetings scheduled. I had a lot of things on my mind, and I didn't remember the note until I changed clothes."

"You still could have given it to them," Harry insisted, reading the note again. How could he have forgotten to give such an important piece of evidence to the police? Had he truly been as upset as all that, or had he withheld it purposely? And if so, why? What motive would he have had to interfere in a seemingly straightforward suicide investigation, especially since he claimed he had never met Gertie before he checked into the Seashore Motel? Did he think the police would be more likely to consider Gertie's death a murder if there was no suicide note? But why would he want them to think it was murder?

"Yeah, sure I could have," he scoffed. "But don't you imagine that if I had trotted down to the police station a couple hours later and handed it to them, that they would have thought I had something to do with it?"

"She committed suicide, Cliff. They would have understood if you'd said you were so upset you just plain forgot about it," Harry pointed out.

"Not Calvin," he said. "He'd just use it against me. Charge me with obstructing justice, or something."

"Don't be absurd," Harry replied. "They've closed the case, so why would they bother charge you with anything?"

"If they closed the case, then they don't need it, do they? So why should I put my neck on the line?" he rationalized.

"That's not the point," Harry said. "You should drop by the police station and give it to them."

"I wouldn't go there again if you paid me a million dollars," Cliff replied firmly, rising from the easy chair. "Not with that right wing bastard looking down his nose at me because I'm gay. Look, if you're so worried about it, *you* give it to them. I've signed my statement, and as soon as the sun comes up, I'm out of here. And I don't care if I ever see this wretched town again."

"Cliff —"

"Look, do what you want. It's unfortunate that you showed up when you did or no one would have been any the wiser," he said. "You must have guessed by now that I came back here tonight to drop off the note. Not on the table, that would have been too obvious. I was going to put it a kitchen cupboard or under the edge of the carpet. I hadn't decided yet when you came along. You can leave it here, give it to the police, flush it down the toilet, or keep it as a souvenir. I don't care. Just stop bugging me."

"What made you think that Gertie was murdered, especially after you found this note?" Harry asked quietly.

He grimaced, and then looked sheepish. "I never really thought she was murdered. I just wanted to get you off my back."

"Really," Harry said sceptically.

"It's the truth," he protested. "I was scared shitless when you walked in. I mean, what if it had been the cops? And what if you were some upstanding citizen ready to sic the police on me for keeping this note?"

"Tell me the truth, Cliff. Why didn't you turn it in?" Harry asked insistently.

"I don't know," he shrugged. "When the cops arrived, they seemed so callous. They didn't care. They walked around with cigarettes hanging out their mouths, talked about what they had for dinner the night before and made jokes while they were taking pictures of her body and searching the apartment. It was just another job for them, one to finish as soon as possible so they could go off duty and slug back a couple of beers. It didn't seem right. So I just never got around to giving it to them. Call it a poor man's revenge, if you like. Of course it didn't take me long to realize that I'd been stupid, that I —"

"You knew Gertrude Cashin, didn't you?" Harry asked.

He gave her a hang-dog look. She ignored it. "Well?"

"Why should I tell you anything?" he blustered, pacing the room.

"Why shouldn't you? We're both gay, and neither of us have any particular reason to be fond of the police. And you know as well as I do that Gertie committed suicide, so it's not as if you'd be implicating yourself in a crime," Harry replied reasonably.

He paced.

Harry waited, trying to be patient.

"Some cops are absolutely vicious towards gay men," he said.

"I know that. They aren't exactly enamoured of lesbians, either," she replied.

"You've got to protect yourself, especially when it isn't important," he added.

"And some things aren't important in a case like this, since no crime was committed," she finished for him.

"Precisely," he said, glancing at her.

"Look, I understand exactly what you're saying, although I don't agree with you," Harry said. "But I'm not going to think the worse of you for it. You may as well tell me the truth. It won't go any further."

"But why does it matter to you? You didn't even know her," he said.

"It's important to me, that's all," Harry responded.

He stopped pacing. He had made a decision.

"My sales territory takes in all of New England," he began. "I used to come down here at least twice a year, sometimes more often, depending on business. But I despise travelling. It's enervating. It takes you away from home, and it's hard to make friends or to find — and especially keep — a lover. More often than not, the mattresses are too soft and the food stinks, but your travel budget doesn't cover first class hotels and four star restaurants. So you learn to sniff out comfortable places which don't cost a lot."

"And the Seashore Motel was one of them," Harry surmised.

"Yes."

"How long had you been coming here?"

"For at least ten years," he replied.

"And you didn't think the police would find out?" Harry asked incredulously.

"I didn't think they'd bother do too much digging," he said with a shrug. "Not when they found out that she had killed herself."

"You've got some nerve, lying like that," Harry retorted.

He grinned sheepishly. "Like I told you, I didn't want to get involved. But obviously, I knew Gertie. She'd chat me up each time I arrived, although that was business. I was a repeat customer, and she didn't want to lose me to any of the big chains, which were also offering comfort for cheap. It just so happens that I prefer older motels. They're more homey, and they don't all look the same. So she didn't have to worry, but she didn't know that. She never came right out and told me, but I knew she was a lesbian. It would have been pretty hard to miss. Sometimes she'd ask me in for a drink, but we never talked about that. I never learned anything about her private life. She didn't say, and I didn't ask."

"So what did you think when you found out that she had disappeared?" Harry asked.

"Believe it or not, I never heard a thing about it," he replied.

Harry looked sceptical.

"It's the truth!" he protested. "I used to come down here twice a year, but when the recession took hold, I often skipped the Cape altogether and spent all of my time in Boston. That was where most of my business was anyway. I guess I hadn't been down to the Cape in, oh, more than a year when I decided to give it another try. When I got here, the motel was half-deserted and there was a strange woman in the office. She said she was a relative of Gertie's, and that she was looking after the place until Gertie got better."

"How long ago was that?" Harry asked, leaning forward.

"Oh, four or five years ago," he said vaguely.

"Then it was after Gertie disappeared," Harry said. "And this woman told you that Gertie was sick?"

He nodded. "When I'd been here before, I could see that she was fading, but I thought it was just old age. I asked this relative of hers what was wrong with her, but she didn't want to tell me. She said Gertie didn't want anyone to know."

"Weren't you suspicious?" Harry asked.

"About what?" he responded. "People get sick, and it's not unusual for them to want to keep things private. I was a stranger, after all, somebody who rented a room once in a while. And this woman didn't know me from Adam."

"How old was she? What did she look like?"

"You don't want much, do you?" he said with a laugh. "She was middle-aged. Dark hair. Attractive, I suppose. And I'm nearly certain she was a lesbian. Maybe it runs in the family."

"Was she here every time you came down?" Harry asked.

He nodded. "But don't forget, I haven't been here that often in the past five years. Three times, maybe. Anyway, what's the big deal?"

He was right, Harry thought. Gertie had disappeared, and one of her relatives had taken over the running of the motel. Perhaps Gertie's family, of which she knew nothing except that Kate's ex-lover Lila was a niece, had thought that Gertie would return soon, and that they would manage the motel for her until she did. What could be more natural? Family members did that for each other. Who could have known that it would stretch into five years? And the family wouldn't want every Tom, Dick and Harry staying at the motel to know that Gertie had disappeared. Guests would ask questions they couldn't answer, and it might prove to be bad for business.

Harry sighed; she was obviously making a mountain out of a molehill.

"Are you finished cross-examining me?" Cliff asked dryly.

"Are you sure you don't know anything else?" she asked suspiciously.

"What's there to know?" he said with a grin.

"At least take this note to the police station on your way out of town," she requested, holding out the letter.

"Not on your life," he said emphatically. "Like I said, do what you want with it. I don't care."

And that was that, Harry thought, watching him leave the apartment. She heard the slam of the outside door, and shortly after, the sound of a motor being revved. She had lots of gay male friends, but Cliff was certainly not her kind of guy. He played too loosely with the truth. It would have been a simple matter for him to have given Gertie's suicide note to the police, and to have explained that he knew Gertie because he had often rented rooms at the Seashore Motel in the course of his work. While his failure to do so probably hadn't created any problems in the police investigation of Gertie's death, lying hadn't served any real purpose, either. He would never have been considered a suspect in her disappearance, so why hadn't he divulged the truth? Harry didn't think he had been afraid of a little extra questioning by the police, so perhaps his reluctance had been caused by a certain moral carelessness, a form of ethical laxity. Cliff was lazy, that was all. He didn't want to bother. Him and most of the rest of the world, Harry thought sardonically, rising from the chair.

She read the note again, refolded it carefully, and tucked it in the zipper compartment of her purse.

Traffic had thinned, so she didn't have long to wait to cross the road. She jogged swiftly across the grass to the motel, shivering in the damp, late-night air. Gertie's last known communication to the world, a missive which the devious Cliff Jones had withheld from the police, a message which she was now concealing, seemed to weigh her down. Her purse hung heavily on her shoulder and battered her hip. She told herself that she would behave better than Cliff, that she would give Gertie's note to the police. Soon. Otherwise it might burst into flame or explode in her face. She opened the door, entered her room, and took out the suicide note.

"The time has come," she read, crossing the carpeted floor. Harry shuddered and wondered if she would be brave enough to stare death in the face without blinking. Gertie, courageous to the end, had literally smiled, opened the door, and invited death in. Harry had the feeling that she would bellow in anger and roar with defiance until she had no more breath left in her body, but who was to say which was more valiant? To want to live was nothing to be ashamed of, although perhaps the inability to face death once it became inevitable was. But why had that particular night been the appropriate time to die? Why not some other time? Had Gertie been in such agony that she couldn't bear to linger for another second, or had she been waiting for something to happen?

Perhaps "All has been resolved" was the answer to that question. Gertie had chosen to die when she did because it was the right time, and it was the right time because something had been resolved. But what? Gertie wasn't telling.

And then she had written, "Do not wonder where I was, it is of no consequence now." Gertie had disappeared for a reason, one which she wasn't going to share with the police, although she must have known that they would be interested in solving that particular mystery. But think, now. Gertie believed that the police would find her note when they discovered her body, the empty pill bottle, the mug, the bottle of brandy. Why did she maintain that her disappearance was "of no consequence" when it was likely related to the reason she had chosen to die when she did? And why had she added the word "now"? Would there have been consequences if the reason for her disappearance or her hiding place had been discovered earlier? Or, for that matter, if she had died earlier? Would those consequences have been importune? Would people, including Gertie, have been in trouble? Had they been involved in something illegal, as Judy had postulated? It was like a riddle, circling back on itself to mock her deductive abilities. Only someone who knew why Gertie had disappeared and where she had been could possibly understand such cryptic language.

"Do not question what has happened, I have made this decision of my own free will." At least that seemed straightforward, as did, "Do not ponder the involvement of others, for there has been none." Gertie was absolving others of responsibility in her death, affirming that she had made a rational decision to end her life, and that she had done it by herself. But why had she been afraid that someone would be blamed? Had she had help, but wanted the police to believe otherwise?

Harry walked to the window and stared across the road at the Seashore Motel, willing it to give up its secrets. What a crafty suicide note. On the one hand, it was simplicity personified. It conveyed the impression that Gertie had unquestionably done the right thing at the right time. On the other hand, it was devious, nearly Machiavellian. To the initiated, whoever they were, Gertie had penned an enigmatic message that she had succeeded in carrying out whatever secret deed she had undertaken to accomplish five years before. Harry wondered how long it had taken Gertie to compose the note. Had she sat there in her chair, pen poised over paper, the bottle of pills and a mug of brandy on the table beside her, smiling at this last bit of deviltry? Or had she simply scribbled something without too much thought?

No matter, Harry thought. All this idle speculation wasn't going to lead anywhere, because she would never know what had been in Gertie's mind. Nevertheless, the suicide note troubled her. Despite the fact that she was dying of cancer, Gertie hadn't mentioned her illness as a motivating factor in her suicide.

She was still staring out the window, deep in thought, when Kate pulled up in her red convertible.

"Oh, lord!" Harry exclaimed. She hastily folded the note, tucked it in her purse, and went out.

"Hi!" Kate said. "I see you're still up."

"Yes," Harry replied, confirming the obvious.

"I guess you're surprised to see me," Kate added.

"Yes," Harry admitted. Surprised and chagrined, not to mention contrite about Gertie's suicide note. "It's late."

"I'm sorry. I couldn't sleep. I couldn't stop thinking about what happened," Kate said. "Look, I'm sorry I rushed you, because I'd rather be friends than nothing at all."

"I see," Harry replied, taken aback.

"Sex isn't everything," Kate added.

Although it sometimes seemed to be, Harry thought.

"So. Can we agree to be friends?" Kate said with a smile, holding out her hand.

"Of course," Harry replied. Kate's palm was warm but dry, her skin soft. Harry was reluctant to release her hand. A woman who knew how to turn on the charm in such a sophisticated manner didn't need to do much else to succeed, Harry thought wryly, her initial attraction to Kate returning more forcefully than ever.

"So how about a belated dinner?" Kate asked, removing her hand from Harry's.

"I'm not sure," Harry replied, thinking of Gertie's suicide note. Kate was a cop, Harry a witness withholding evidence. Harry knew she should give the note to Kate, but her reluctance to part with it increased with each passing second, as did her anxiety. Her hand fluttered nervously to her purse, then moved away. Give it to the cops, Cliff had said, or keep it as a souvenir. It was not the souvenir of Cape Cod that she had had in mind, but it didn't seem like an auspicious moment to confess to Kate. It was too complicated, she rationalized. She would give the note to Calvin in the morning. After all, if it had waited this long, it could wait a little longer, she thought, assuaging her guilt.

"Why not?" Kate asked.

"I'm pretty tired —"

The amused expression on Kate's face stopped her cold. But there were other just as legitimate reasons for her reluctance to accept Kate's invitation, including the fact that she didn't know why Kate had refused to answer all her questions about Gertie.

"We could talk," Kate suggested. "Get to know each other better. And we could continue our conversation of earlier this evening."

"All right," Harry replied. The possibility that Kate would be more forthcoming about Gertie's past prompted her to get into the car, although she realized it hadn't been the only or even the most important reason she had agreed to have dinner with Kate. She recognized the look on Kate's face, a look of hunger for something more than food. She wondered if that look was reflected on her own face, but she was too apprehensive to pull down the sun visor and look in the mirror. Somewhere in the back of her mind, where it had been safe from denial, analysis and rational defeat, Harry had known that their abortive sexual encounter earlier in the evening had been the beginning rather than the end. They could be friends, but they were too attracted to each other to remain only friends, and she was sure that Kate knew this as well as she did. Getting into the car had been an gesture of complicity, an agreement to follow their mutual attraction to its natural conclusion. So while Judy was exploring the possibility of a non-monogamous relationship with her mind, she was embarking on an exploration of the very same thing with her body.

"I'm glad," Kate said, resting her hand on Harry's thigh, which began to tingle pleasantly.

Cliff's vexatious assertion that the police knew more than they were telling popped into Harry's mind. She impatiently shooed it away.

"You're awfully quiet," Kate commented. "A penny for your thoughts."

Harry laughed uncomfortably. "There're not worth half of that."

"And here I was willing to pay a quarter," Kate joked.

"I bet you say that to all the girls," Harry shot back, eliciting a laugh from Kate.

"If only you knew," Kate replied ruefully.

"Tell me," Harry asked, covering Kate's hand with her own, feeling the electricity crackle between them.

"Sometime," Kate said lightly as she drove the car into the driveway, parked and turned it off. "I'm starving," she replied, jumping over the door.

Harry threw caution to the wind and hopped over the passenger-side door, bruising her hip on the protruding mirror. She resisted the urge to give the car a swift kick and followed Kate into her apartment.

"Chinese?" Kate asked, going to the telephone.

"Great. Anything I can do?" Harry asked.

"You could set up the tables," Kate suggested.

Harry opened the TV-tables, placing one in front of the chair and the other in front of the bed.

"And pour some wine," Kate added, removing dishes from the cupboard over the sink and cutlery from one of the drawers.

Harry took two wine glasses from Kate and placed them on the tables.

"It's in the fridge," Kate told her.

Harry moved past Kate and opened the fridge, which was empty except for a carton of milk, several small containers of yoghurt, a half-eaten iceberg lettuce and a six-pack of beer. She reached in and took out the bottle of wine they had opened earlier in the evening, uncorked it, and filled their wine glasses.

"To the future," Kate murmured.

Their glasses touched like skin on skin.

Harry felt herself moving toward the bed, Kate's sultry determination evoking an equally fevered response in her. Kate kissed her, and Harry grew aroused. They fell back on the bed, their bodies coming together. Kate kissed her again, so deep and hard that Harry saw stars. They came up for breath by mutual consent, and Harry suddenly wondered what Judy would do in this situation, how she would handle temptation so strong that it threatened to completely overwhelmed her senses. Silly question, she thought. She *knew* what Judy had done; she had made love with Lorna. It seemed that this was now permitted.

Then the doorbell rang.

"Oh god," Kate moaned. "It's the delivery man."

"I'm not hungry," Harry whispered.

"Like hell you're not," Kate said with a wicked grin. She raised herself from Harry's body, running her fingers lightly between Harry's legs. "You're wet right through your pants."

The doorbell rang again, sending both of them scampering from the bed. While Kate found her wallet and opened the door to pay for their dinner, Harry retreated to the bathroom, locking the door behind her. She needed time to compose herself. Whatever it took to arouse Harry, it was something which Kathleen Yokes had in abundance.

Did she want this sort of complication in her life? What if she was starting something she didn't want to end? She should compose herself, march resolutely out there, and play it cool. She should sip wine cautiously, eat Chinese food until her stomach bulged, and ask all those questions about Gertie which she hadn't had the chance to put to Kate earlier in the evening. And then she should leave. Yes, so she should.

"Are you going to hide in there all night?"

Harry sighed. "Coming," she called, opening the door and returning to the room.

Kate was smiling. Harry avoided looking directly at her, but the smile followed her around the room. The bedspread and top sheet had been turned down.

"Where's dinner?" she asked, looking at the counters, which were bare. The TV-tables were folded and standing upright against the wall.

"Later," Kate said. "We've got something else to finish first."

It was foolish to fight it. Desire propelled Harry into Kate's arms, and they returned to the bed. Harry sank into the demanding sensuality of Kate's mouth, knowing that this time there would be no doorbell, no delivery man, no possibility of interruption unless she requested it. Kate took the lead, peeling Harry's clothes from her body, then removing her own, tossing everything to the floor. They kissed, their lips wet, their tongues exploring. Kate's mouth was cool and tasted of wine. Kate's breasts were small, exquisite, responsive, her thighs muscular. And she was wet too. Harry felt hands cup her breasts, measuring their size, their shape, then concentrating on bringing her nipples to full erection, stroking them relentlessly until they ached. She wanted to cry out for Kate to have mercy, to push her away but not too far away and not for very long, to stop or at least mitigate the intense longing which was consuming her body. But her own desire made her powerless to stop Kate or her own response to this woman's lovemaking. Her skin was fevered with desire; her breasts felt swollen with need, and Kate's fingers were swooping down over her belly and boldly cupping her mons. Long, silky touches inflamed her, and a sharp, prolonged orgasm shook her body. Kate came a few moments later.

Harry broke away, breathing heavily, her heart thumping rapidly.

"Ever do it like this?" Kate asked gruffly, climbing on top of her and sliding her thigh between Harry's.

Harry groaned at the pleasurable friction as Kate thrust against her. Heat was building in her belly again, but she didn't know if she could have another orgasm so soon after the first.

"Don't rush. I don't care how long it takes," Kate whispered in her ear just before she tongued it.

Harry relaxed, letting Kate control the rhythm. And it was a good rhythm too, rocking her gently, slowly, giving her senses time to revive. They kissed languidly and for a long time, until Harry could feel the wet flesh between her thighs engorge. Kate must have felt it too, because she increased the speed of her movements and her thigh rubbed harder against Harry.

Harry broke their kiss to gasp for breath, and then moaned as a long, drawn-out orgasm shook her.

"Good," Kate gasped, and then Harry felt Kate's hand slide down between them. Fingers slid deep into her vagina and began plunging in and out.

"No —"

"Shh," Kate whispered, moving more gently inside her.

Harry's vagina was open and lubricated, easily accepting Kate's fingers, but she had never enjoyed being penetrated. Her hips stilled.

"You don't like this?" Kate asked, slowing further.

"No."

"Not usually, you mean," Kate said with a soft laugh. "Why don't you try?"

Kate's fingers were barely moving now, and her thumb had moved up to cover Harry's clitoris.

"I don't know if I can come again," Harry said weakly.

"Never mind," Kate said, withdrawing her hand from between Harry's thighs. "That last time felt like a major eruption, anyway."

Major eruption, Harry thought? Well, she supposed that was as good a way as any to describe it. Her body was covered with sweat, and her pubic area felt as if it had been scrubbed clean by a dust storm.

"Here, let's get under the covers," Kate suggested, standing up beside the bed and tugging at the dishevelled bedspread and sheets.

"I really should be going," Harry protested, but she let herself be tucked in. Kate slid in beside her and wrapped her body around her spoon-fashion. It felt good.

"Let's have a little nap. We can eat when we wake up. All we'll have to do is heat it up in the microwave."

Oh yes, dinner. Chinese food. Harry closed her eyes and fell asleep thinking about how hungry she was.

"This is a pretty kettle of fish," Gertie commented. She was sitting in an easy chair in her living room, dressed in a cerise, '30s-style dressing gown, the ubiquitous brandy snifter in one hand and a lit, smelly cigarillo in the other. She looked like a debonair lesbian libertine.

"I didn't know you smoked," Harry replied. She was in the other easy chair, and there was a full brandy snifter on the end table. She didn't bother taste it — she was certain it was rum.

"Only when I'm having fun," Gertie said dryly, blowing smoke in her direction.

Harry coughed.

"I suppose you're allergic to smoke, too," Gertie added disparagingly.

Harry didn't dignify that comment with an reply. "So tell me; what's so pretty about this particular kettle of fish?"

"You haven't listened to anything I've said, have you?" Gertie scolded.

Harry picked up her brandy snifter and had some rum. Really, she wasn't in the mood for this tonight.

"That's gratitude for you," Gertie said with a sigh. "I could have left you sitting there stark naked the way you were born, but I thought it might bother you. Heaven knows why, you haven't got anything different from any other woman in this world, but there it is. False modesty."

Harry couldn't resist looking down at herself. She was dressed in an unflattering dressing gown which was too small for her. She tugged the ends together and belted it more firmly around her middle.

"I was simply trying to help," Gertie said.

Her tone was mild, but Harry knew she was annoyed. "I listened to what you said," she replied meekly.

"But did you understand any of it?"

"Your girlfriend left you for a man and never came back," Harry said, taking another drink of rum.

"Simplistic but not incorrect," Gertie responded.

"And you pined for her until the day you died," Harry added.

"Melodramatic, but again, not entirely incorrect," Gertie replied. "And what, my dear Harriet, have you learned from this, if anything?"

"That there are some similarities," Harry said reluctantly.

"Between what and what? Elucidate, my dear woman," Gertie encouraged her.

"Your situation and mine," Harry said with some bitterness.

"Are there, now?"

"Maybe."

Gertie snorted and finished her brandy. "You're a slow drinker," she commented.

"I don't want to get drunk," Harry replied.

"You won't have a hangover," Gertie assured her, pouring brandy into her snifter from the bottle on the end table. "You know, my dear, you shouldn't be surprised when you discover similarities. Relationships are always similar, just as they're always different. I was in an awful state when Vera moved to California, married that young pup and never came back. I was desperate. Heartbroken. My pride was severely damaged. And of course I had never been with another woman, and the thought of finding someone else in those closeted days was daunting, even to someone like me," Gertie said.

"What did you do?" Harry asked, taking a drink now that Gertie wasn't pressuring her.

"What every young, hot-blooded lesbian would do: I wrote her letters. Love letters, heartsick letters, passionate letters, rude letters, angry letters, pity-me letters. In rotation, depending on how I felt on any given day. Sometimes I wanted to throttle her, sometimes all I could think of was how much I missed her. But it was no use. All my letters were returned unopened," Gertie said.

"Didn't you ever think of going out there after her?"

"Constantly," Gertie replied.

"Then why didn't you?"

"I was afraid to," Gertie said simply.

Harry was shocked.

"I was a proud, vain woman," Gertie explained. "I was afraid that she would reject me."

"What happened then?" Harry asked.

"Oh, what happened is what usually happens. Life goes on," Gertie replied with a lopsided smile. "The motel kept me busy. And I began to travel regularly to Boston for companionship."

"You took lovers?" Harry asked incredulously.

"Don't look so perturbed," Gertie said with a laugh. "Did you think I spent the rest of my life on the shelf? Do I seem like the type to be celibate?"

Harry opened her mouth and closed it again.

"Honestly, young people can be so idealistic," Gertie muttered to herself. "Or thoughtless. Or both. You're not the only one with needs, Harriet. Although, unlike you, I waited a decent amount of time until I went looking for someone else."

"That's not fair," Harry protested.

"Fair? Who said that life was fair?" Gertie scoffed. "Do you think Judy will think you were fair, for example? Or that you're taking her need for solitude seriously if you can't do without female companionship for one night?"

Harry drained her brandy snifter, put the empty glass on the table, and waited for her dream to end. It didn't.

"You have to learn to think things through," Gertie told her. "Otherwise, you're going to end up like me."

"Judy started it first," Harry muttered defensively.

"Now, now," Gertie laughed. "You know better than that. Have another drink."

Why was it that in her dreams she was always getting drunk, Harry wondered as she rose unsteadily from the chair and took the brandy bottle from Gertie. "Well, she did," she asserted. "She left me for no good reason."

"Oh, she had her reasons," Gertie replied.

"So what were they?" Harry asked belligerently, filling her brandy snifter.

"She told you, Harriet," Gertie said gently, "but I don't think you listened."

"I did too," Harry whined.

"Or understood," Gertie added, unperturbed by Harry's self-pity.

"You certainly have a high opinion of me," Harry commented bitterly, taking a swig of rum.

"High enough to be here with you," Gertie said, "although sometimes I wonder why I bother."

Harry squinted drunkenly at the elderly woman sitting across from her. Her expression was one of what, Harry wondered? Amusement? Affection? Disappointment?

"If you would only think, Harry," Gertie admonished. "Think, and it will become clear to you."

What did Gertie imagine she had been doing the past couple of days?

"Think, I said, not react."

She *had* been thinking! She had! But it was like trying to wrestle a greased pig to the ground or conversing with someone who spoke another language or attempting to find the source of that damn noise ...

14

"What the hell ...?"

"Don't worry, it's just my radio alarm. It's early, so go back to sleep if you like," Kate said, stretching.

"It's morning?" Harry exclaimed, watching Kate walk across the room to the bathroom and close the door. Then she glanced out the window, which was partially covered by curtains that looked suspiciously like terry-cloth towels. It was foggy; she could barely make out the shape of the building next door, but it was light enough for her to see that it was dawn.

She hadn't meant to sleep right through the night, but after such vigorous sex, even her dream hadn't roused her. She hoped fervently that Judy hadn't dropped by their motel room to pick up her clothes. What would she have thought when she found their room empty? Oh lord, what a quandary. She scrambled from the bed and pawed swiftly through the clothes on the floor, pulling on her panties and bra and then her wrinkled sweatshirt and slacks, waiting impatiently for Kate to vacate the bathroom.

"You're dressed already?" Kate said with surprise when she reentered the room. "I thought we might go back to bed for a bit and then have breakfast together. I always set the clock early to have a little time for myself in the morning, so I don't have to leave for work right away," she added, disappointment written plainly on her face.

"I should get back to the motel," Harry replied, wavering. Try as she might, she was unable to keep her eyes from Kate's well-built and still nude body. She was simply gorgeous. But her preoccupation with Kate's attractiveness had caused her downfall in the first place. It had distracted her from her purpose, which had been to closely question Kate about Gertie.

"Are you worried about your lover?"

Harry looked away and nodded. Yes, she was troubled about Judy, not to mention her distress about Gertie's note.

"Oh, well," Kate said lightly. "There's always the next time. I'll get breakfast ready. At least you can stay long enough for that, can't you?"

With a guilty nod, Harry walked past Kate and entered the bathroom, using the toilet and splashing some hot water on her face. She would have preferred to have a shower and wash the smell of sweat, of arousal, of Kate's body, from her own, but she didn't want to take the time. She finger-combed her hair and then gave up. Her cowlick was going to win today, and she didn't give a damn.

She scrutinized herself in the mirror and grimaced. She looked hungover, which was ludicrous. It had merely been a nightmare, a dream in which Gertie had made typically cryptic comments, while she, as usual, had imbibed too much neat rum. But dream or not, Gertie was serving as a vigilant conscience, or perhaps more correctly, as a reflection of her subconscious. It was the proverbial morning after. She felt removed from the situation, and this detachment made her feel strange, as if she were observing while her alter ego performed. Whatever had possessed her to suddenly jettison years of fidelity? Had she temporarily lost her mind?

She was also withholding evidence from the very police officer with whom she had gone to bed. While she and Kate had been locked in passionate combat, Gertie's suicide note had been ticking like a time bomb in her purse. She should have given the note to Kate as soon as they met, because she definitely couldn't now. It would be impossible to justify the delay, especially when she couldn't provide a satisfactory explanation for it to herself.

She stared at her frowning image in the mirror.

"Breakfast is ready," Kate shouted through the closed door.

"Coming," Harry muttered. She gave her cowlick one last pat before opening the door.

Kate was dressed in her police uniform, a holstered gun on her hip. "Kiss me," she said with a grin.

She was kissing a cop before breakfast. A cop wearing a gun. Kate pulled her close and gave her a second, harder kiss, sending her sense of the absurd flying. "I like you," she said gruffly.

Harry nodded, feeling close to tears.

"Let's eat," Kate said.

Harry sat down, grateful to Kate for pretending not to notice.

"I hope you don't mind Chinese food," Kate remarked. "I eat anything anytime, I guess it comes with the job and never knowing when I'm going to be called out for an emergency. Sometimes I forget that other people have definite ideas about what's suitable for breakfast, lunch or dinner."

"This is fine," Harry said, breaking an egg roll with her fork. "Kate, did your ex-lover look after the Seashore Motel when Gertie disappeared?"

Kate dropped her fork on the floor and sat there staring at it. "I guess I'd better get a clean one," she mumbled, rising from the bed.

That was illuminating, Harry thought as she watched Kate walk across the room, open a drawer and take out a fork.

"Who told you?" Kate asked as she sat down without looking at Harry.

"No one," Harry fibbed, disconcerted about what a good liar she was becoming. "It just seemed logical. The motel stayed open for five years after Gertie disappeared, so someone had to be taking care of business. I thought it was likely to have been a relative, and Lila is the only one I know about."

"Yes, it was Lila," Kate replied evenly, pushing her plate away. "I seem to have lost my appetite."

"And did you help sometimes?"

"No," Kate said. "Lila did everything."

"Even after she moved to Boston?" Harry asked, continuing to eat. She was starved, and the chicken fried rice, the sweet and sour beef and the vegetable chow mein were delicious.

"It got harder for Lila to do everything once she was in Boston, so I did a few things once in a while," Kate admitted. "Lila was only here on weekends, so the place was empty most of the time. Before that, she went there almost every night right after work and stayed late, renting out rooms, cleaning, keeping the books, doing the banking, paying the bills. Somebody had to do it, otherwise there wouldn't have been enough money to pay the taxes, the electrical bill, the laundry bill — you have no idea how much it costs to keep a motel afloat. Lila either had to keep the motel running or close it down. She couldn't sell it. She couldn't do anything much except keep it open, not while Gertie was missing."

"Was Lila her only relative?" Harry asked, placing her knife and fork across her empty plate.

"Yes," Kate nodded. "The only one I knew of, anyway. Gertie was the baby of the family, and all her brothers and sisters moved away a long time ago. Most of them are dead now. Lila was born when her mother was in her mid-forties, and she was the only child. There might be a few cousins around, but Lila never mentioned them."

"And she and Gertie were close," Harry said.

"Lila's mother passed away when Lila was in her early teens," Kate said. "Gertie took her in until she was old enough to look after herself."

"So Lila lived with Gertie?"

"Yes," Kate confirmed. "Gertie fixed up one of the rooms for her, the one closest to the office."

"Then Lila learned the business while she was growing up," Harry said.

"Gertie wanted her to take over when she retired, but Lila had other ideas," Kate said. "She didn't mind helping, but she found the motel business limiting. You have to be there all the time, work long hours, deal with people you wouldn't necessarily choose to meet. And you never get to take a vacation. Come to think of it, the career Lila did choose isn't much different."

"Did Gertie leave the motel to Lila?" Harry asked.

"She intended to, so I imagine she did," Kate replied. "But I don't know for sure; Lila and I haven't talked much since we broke up."

"If Gertie and Lila were that close, why didn't Gertie tell Lila where she was going, and why?" Harry asked.

"How should I know?" Kate said, shifting restlessly. "Look, Gertie always was a bit of a gadfly. Sometimes she would take off for Boston without so much as a word of warning, and she'd stay away for weeks at a time, even when Lila was still a kid. Most of the time she would call a few days later and apologize for not leaving a note. I thought that was a bit much, but Lila was used to it. Anyway, we both knew that she was, to put it bluntly, in need of a romp in the hay on a regular basis. She refused to consider dating anybody in West Yarmouth; she said it would lead to too many complications in her life. I don't think she ever wanted a serious relationship, she was afraid it would tie her down."

"So when she disappeared five years ago, you thought she was off on another one of her escapades," Harry said.

"That's right," Kate said. "She didn't call, but that wasn't unusual. We didn't start to get worried until a couple of weeks went by and we still hadn't heard from her."

"What did you do then?"

"Lila and I contacted some of her friends in Boston, but none of them had heard from her in months, and she certainly wouldn't have gone to Boston without calling someone. Especially since she was so sick, so weak. She would have needed help to get around. Actually, I was surprised that she had the energy to pick up and go anywhere, but Gertie was quite strong-willed. Anyway, at that point, Lila formally notified the police that her aunt was missing," Kate replied.

"And they did nothing," Harry commented, forgetting for a moment that Kate was a cop even though she was wearing her uniform.

"Not precisely," Kate said sarcastically, her eyes meeting Harry's momentarily. "Look, I told you before that there's no law against an adult taking off, and if they want to stay missing, they usually can. Hell, even when we find them, we can't tell their relatives where they are if they don't want us to."

"Did you think she'd turn up before long?" Harry asked, wishing she had a cup of coffee but not wanting to interrupt Kate.

"Of course," Kate replied. "What else could we believe? She was seriously ill. She was finding it hard to manage at home without outside help. So even though we couldn't figure out where she went, we thought she'd come back before long."

"But she didn't," Harry said softly.

"No."

"What do you think happened?"

Kate stared stonily at her.

"You must have some idea," Harry prodded.

"None whatsoever," Kate said with finality.

"But —"

"Lila either," she added, looking at her watch. "I'd better get going or I'll be late for work."

Harry suppressed her annoyance and helped Kate rinse their dishes and stack them in the sink, and fold the TV-tables and lean them in their customary place against the wall.

"I didn't mean to cut you off, Harry. It's just that it's still hard for me to talk about this," Kate said as she wiped her hands on a towel.

"It's okay," Harry replied. And it was also true, she realized. In the past two weeks, Kate had lost Lila and Gertie, her lover and a good friend, and that would be painful for anyone to discuss. But Harry had the feeling there was something more on Kate's mind, something unsaid which she wanted to share but couldn't. She had had the same sensation when she had been questioning Cliff in Gertie's apartment in the Seashore Motel. It was like an itch at the back of her brain, a hunch, or intuition, perhaps. She was almost certain that Kate was keeping something from her. It was futile to pry, though; Kate wasn't going to disclose anything else, not now. Harry turned away, picked up her purse and headed for the door.

"I'll drop you at your motel," Kate said as they left the apartment. Harry got into the convertible. Kate hopped over the door, turned her key in the ignition, pulled out from the curb and drove down the street.

The fog was pervasive. Harry felt like she had been wrapped in a wet blanket. The seats were damp, and the windscreen was coated with moisture which coalesced and dripped slowly on the dashboard, forming little puddles on the plastic.

So much for this particular romance, Harry thought ruefully; passion had shrivelled like a water-starved berry once they had started to talk about Gertie. So had her ability to banter creatively; she was obsessed with Gertie, with Lila's relationship with Gertie, with Kate's relationship with Gertie, with Gertie's disappearance and death.

"Will we see each other again?" Kate asked as she sped around a corner.

"I don't know how long I'm going to be here," Harry replied, thinking about Judy. There would be discordant music to face, but if their relationship was to survive, face it she must.

"It's not only that, is it?" Kate said, glancing at her.

Of course it wasn't, Harry thought, looking away. There was also Gertie's suicide note, Cliff's confession that he had known Gertie, and her guilt about keeping both of those things from Kate.

"I know. You don't have to say anything," Kate said with a sigh.

"Sorry," Harry muttered. In one night, she had managed to deceive — and betray — everyone she cared about.

"Here we are," Kate said, pulling into the parking lot of the motel. "Look, don't answer now," she said, putting the car in park and turning to Harry.

"But —"

"You never know," Kate said, and then she shrugged and laughed. "Oh, hell, I guess it's just wishful thinking."

Harry was touched by her rather awkward honesty, and put her hand on Kate's arm. "You know that I can't promise anything."

"Of course not," Kate responded. "It would be a miracle if you could. Or a lie," she added sardonically. "Anyway, I've got to get to work."

"Kate, I didn't mean to hurt you," Harry blurted. "Or to pry."

"Hurt me?" Kate queried with a cryptic glance. "Oh, you didn't hurt me."

Harry waited for more, but Kate was silent. "Good," she said, trying not to sound as confused as she felt.

"The funeral is this afternoon," Kate said suddenly, as if she had just come to a decision.

"Gertie's?" Harry asked.

"Honestly, Harry," Kate said with a sad smile. "Who did you think? I'd like you to come."

"I'll be there, then," Harry said firmly, although she hated funerals. She had detested them ever since her parents had forced her to attend the funeral of her grandfather when she was so small that she had to be lifted up to kiss him on the cheek. She could still remember his cold, pallid skin, the artificial smell of the cosmetics which coated his face and the dreadful wrongness of it all, especially when the pot-bellied funeral director had casually closed the lid of the casket on her grandfather's face. She had started to scream then, and her mother had taken her home, her own grief blocking compassion for her child's terror. She had scolded Harry for her outburst, and Harry had absorbed this cruel lesson. She came to understand that Protestant practices were repressive. It was acceptable to cry quietly but not to make a scene, to mourn unemotionally in order not to inconvenience others. Restraint in everything was the preferred way.

"I'm glad you can come," Kate said, and then she kissed her, but it was nothing more than a polite touching of lips. Harry got out of the car, debating with herself as she closed the door. She could still do something right. She could give Gertie's suicide letter to Kate and tell her about Cliff Jones, but as she and Kate stared at each other, she realized that she was not going to do either. There was still too much of the cat and mouse about this, and until she was certain whether she was the cat or the mouse, she wasn't going to do a thing.

"Kate," she said, leaning over the side.

"What?"

"Who was Vera?"

Kate's mouth dropped open. "How on earth did you know about her?"

"Don't ask," Harry replied, her stomach churning. "She was Gertie's lover, wasn't she? In the old days."

"In the *very* old days. Back when Gertie was young," Kate replied, looking at Harry with suspicion. "That's ancient history, Harry. How did you know? Have you been asking around? Or did Gertie tell you?"

Harry saved herself by nodding.

"She hadn't talked about that in years," Kate muttered, biting her lip. "Why would she tell a stranger? And why didn't you mention it in your interview with Calvin?"

"I didn't want to say anything about Gertie being a lesbian," Harry said, wishing for a multitude of reasons that she hadn't been stupid enough to mention Vera.

"Calvin knew," Kate replied evenly, her eyes cool with distrust.

"How was I supposed to know that?" Harry said, appealing to her.

"It's hard to keep secrets in a small town," Kate answered.

"I don't live in a small town, particularly this one," Harry responded.

"Touché," Kate said.

"I didn't want to mention that I was a lesbian, either," Harry added.

"Oh, I'm sure he knew that, too," Kate responded dryly. "See you at the funeral." She gave Harry quick directions to the cemetery, backed up and drove down the driveway without looking back.

15

What she had discovered in her dreams was true, Harry acknowledged reluctantly. But how could that be? How could she have accurately summoned the past of a stranger while asleep, right down to the name of a long-lost lover? The enormity of it made her tremble, and she realized that her first instinct, to avoid verifying the veracity of her dreams, had been correct. She shouldn't have asked Kate about Vera. She hadn't really needed to know. And now Kate's cop instincts were aroused, and she would probably be much more difficult to question.

Frustrated, Harry kicked a stone sitting forlornly in the middle of the driveway, sending it sailing into the tall witch grass growing in the gutter. She glanced at Bug as she walked toward her motel room, and then stopped in her tracks.

Someone was sitting in the passenger seat of her car. It was early morning, and the windows were steamy with residual night-dew, but she could still discern the distinct shape of a person. "What the hell?" she muttered indignantly. Visions of random acts of violence flitted through her mind, but, enraged that someone had invaded her space, she disregarded them. She was going to be really angry if someone had hurt Bug. She balled her fists and approached her car, then reached out and rapped on the window, ready to create her own version of mayhem, starting with a thorough tongue-lashing.

The window rolled down and she unballed her fists; it was Judy.

"Finally!" her lover exclaimed, lowering the window. "I thought the two of you would never finish."

She had been caught with her proverbial pants down, Harry thought with dismay. She reached in to pull up the door lock and opened the door. Her heart was thumping with fear, shame, guilt —

you name it, she was suffering from it — but Judy seemed impossibly relaxed.

"I just came to get my clothes," she said in a matter-of-fact manner.

"Oh," Harry said. She unlocked the door to her motel room and reached in to switch on the light. She wanted to take Judy in her arms and kiss away their differences, but if this was on Judy's mind, it certainly didn't show. Judy was standing just inside the door, as if there was an invisible line on the carpeted floor which she was reluctant to cross.

"Help yourself," Harry said, perching gingerly on the edge of the bed.

Judy walked across the room and opened the dresser drawer. "You folded everything," she said, obviously surprised.

"Well, yeah," Harry said diffidently.

Judy glanced at her and smiled. "Maybe I should go off on my own more often."

"Heaven forbid!" Harry cried in mock horror, although she felt precisely that way. "Here, let me correct your erroneous impression of me as suzie homemaker incarnate," she said flippantly, rising from the bed and crossing the room. She reached down and removed a pile of neatly folded clothes from the drawer and flung them towards the bed.

"Harry! You idiot!" Judy laughed, grabbing Harry's hands to stop her from repeating this lunacy.

"I want to kiss you," Harry whispered fiercely, squeezing Judy's hands. The smell of her was intoxicating, making Harry's body throb. She wondered how that was possible, given that she had so recently been in bed with Kate.

"I'd like that very much," Judy whispered, closing her eyes.

Harry controlled her passion as their lips met wetly and their and tongues touched. "Oh, I've missed you," she murmured, hugging Judy to her.

"Harry, it's only been a day," Judy reminded her, sounding amused.

"I know, but it felt more like a century," Harry said, kissing her again. She could feel Judy's chuckle and then she stopped thinking about anything except how their bodies fit together and how deep was her love for this woman. "I want you," she muttered, pressing closer.

"Not now, Harry," Judy said, pulling away.

Harry dropped her arms. "Why not?" she asked, her tone gruff.

Judy didn't reply. She returned to the dresser and removed the last pile of her clothes from the drawer.

"Are you going to take everything?" Harry said plaintively, watching Judy pick up the clothes scattered on the floor. "Judy, don't go all silent on me, you know how much I hate that," she complained.

"I'm sorry, Harry," Judy said once she had gathered all her possessions. "Where's my toiletry bag?"

"In the bathroom," Harry said with a defeated sigh. She fell back on the bed and went limp, waiting for Judy to ask about Kate. As if she had to ask, Harry thought wryly. She had seen them arrive at the motel at the crack of dawn, and she had witnessed them kissing in Kate's convertible. No wonder she didn't want to make love.

"I'm going home," Judy said, placing her toiletry bag next to the two neat piles of clothes.

Harry sat up. "What? Back to Montreal?"

"That's right."

"Now? Today?"

"Yes," Kate replied. "Look, you may as well stop looking so stricken. I saw you in her car, I saw the way you were talking with each other, and I saw her kiss you. You don't have to spell it out for me."

"I'm sorry," Harry muttered, wishing she could crawl under the bed and hide.

"I can't say that I'm not upset, but I'm not really surprised. You're attractive to other women, and I sometimes wondered how you resisted temptation, especially since I've been so preoccupied with myself the past few years," Judy told her. "I thought you'd have an affair long before now."

Harry was speechless. "You're not mad at me?"

"Don't ask," Judy warned, laughing bitterly. "I'm as jealous as hell, but of course I haven't the right to be. But if I were a little less charitable, I might presume that you did it out of revenge."

"No," Harry protested, although the thought had entered her mind more than once and she had not been entirely successful in rationalizing it away.

"I'm not going to make excuses for the way I behaved with Lorna, so don't expect me to exonerate you. Let's at least be honest with each other, or as honest as we can be. I don't like how I've cut myself off from you. I haven't been giving you much emotional support, and our sex life has trailed off, too. And that's not the way it should be, certainly not the way I want it to be," Judy said.

"It isn't all that bad," Harry asserted heatedly.

"Nearly," Judy contended. "And yes, of course I'm angry that you slept with that policewoman. I'm human, after all, and I'm just as scared of losing you as you are of losing me. Perhaps it was inevitable that you would find someone else. Maybe it was the only way you could deal with what I did with Lorna. I just hope you didn't do it to punish me."

"Of course I didn't," Harry mumbled.

"I tend to believe you," Judy said. "I think you got involved because she was there and she wanted you, and you couldn't find any good reason to turn her down. I did it first, so why shouldn't you follow suit?"

"But —"

"Let me finish. Because whether we ever talked about it or not, we did have a agreement to remain monogamous," Judy added.

"I felt so ... so —"

"Betrayed," Judy said.

"Yes," Harry replied softly.

"And you probably wouldn't have considered sleeping with someone else if I hadn't got involved with Lorna," Judy said.

"Probably not," Harry said cautiously. She wished Judy would stop flaying it to death. Who knows why one thing happens rather than another? And in the end, what difference did it make? For whatever reasons, they had both been unfaithful. "I don't like what I did, though, or how I did it. And it wasn't worth it," Harry muttered, more to herself than to Judy.

"It rarely is," Judy said with such acerbity that Harry wondered if she was speaking from experience, and if so, whether it was safe to ask about it. She decided that she didn't want to know. Not now, anyway.

"Then why can't you stay? Why can't we just go on from here?" Harry asked.

"Don't you see, I want to like myself again," Judy replied, appealing to Harry for understanding. And patience, which Harry had never been known to possess in great abundance.

"Oh," Harry replied, comprehension dawning. Judy was searching for the holy grail, for deliverance to a state of grace which had eluded the vast majority of people in the world down through history. "And how long is this quest likely to take?" she asked dryly.

"Don't be so cynical. All I want is to regain some of the exuberance I used to feel when I was younger."

"Have you been dissatisfied for a long time?" Harry asked. Judy was talking about a major renovation of her psyche rather than a simple, twice-a-year housecleaning, and that perturbed her.

"No," Judy replied. "Not really. I think I got into a rut, but it's not your fault. Actually, it's nobody's fault. It's just so easy to immerse yourself in work and the stuff of ordinary day-to-day life and lose track of some of the more fundamental things."

But what would happen to their relationship once she reached her goal?

"I just want to be alone for a little longer," Judy said.

Harry had visions of roaming the foggy streets of this tourist trap by herself, supposedly searching for the reason for Gertrude Cashin's disappearance while in reality pining for a woman who professed love but needed solitude to achieve it. She suddenly felt much worse.

"I have to go home, Harry," Judy said. "I need to feel more settled, more at peace."

Harry remained silent.

"You know, I think you've been ignoring one very important factor in this equation," Judy said.

"What?" Harry asked, looking up.

"You."

"Me? What do you mean?"

"Are you assuming that you're going to come out of this completely unchanged?" Judy asked.

"I haven't really thought about it," Harry admitted.

"Well, you should," Judy told her.

Harry watched her get up. Judy was going to leave and there wasn't a damn thing she could do to stop her. "What should I be thinking about?"

"Oh no, I'm not going to do your work for you," Judy said with a laugh as she rapidly tossed her clothes and toiletry bag into the suitcase and zipped it up.

"Well, then, I guess I'll never know what you were talking about," Harry retorted lightly.

"Oh yes you do, and don't you dare try to pretend otherwise. What about Gertrude Cashin? What about your policewoman? And you're having to deal with me, aren't you? Don't try to tell me that these things happen every day," Judy scolded. "Think about it, woman, think about it!"

Harry opened her mouth and closed it again. What the hell did Judy think she had been spending her time doing? She should hear what Harry had discovered, the complex relationships between people, the intrigue, the questions and answers and more questions. It was like peeling an onion, with layer upon layer of facts and personalities and time lines overlapping, spiralling, feeding off each other until she thought she'd go crazy.

"Do you know when you'll be home?" Judy asked.

"I told Kate I'd attend the funeral," Harry replied. "It's this afternoon."

"Are you still trying to get to the bottom of it?" Judy asked, studying Harry's face.

"Yes," Harry said.

"And how's it going?"

"I've got a lot more questions than answers," Harry admitted.

"Red herrings, you mean," Judy commented.

"Red, blue, yellow, orange, you name it," Harry said wryly. "I've found out a lot, but there's still more. People are holding things back."

"People generally do," Judy said with a smile. "But you sound quite sure of that."

"I am," Harry said, and then she realized that she was. Something had gone wrong in West Yarmouth, and she was determined to find out what it was.

"Come home when you're ready, then," Judy whispered, kissing her. "When you're through."

"Yes," Harry said breathlessly. She wished that Judy would shut up and kiss her again.

"I mean it, Harry," Judy said, hugging her. "Take all the time you need. I'll be there when you get back."

"I'll leave tomorrow," Harry promised.

"Shhh," Judy scolded. "I want you to leave when it's over and done with."

"My investigation, you mean," Harry sighed, burying her head in Judy's neck, smelling her warm skin, the familiar brand of suntan lotion she used.

"That and everything else," Judy said, pulling away to look at Harry.

Harry nodded, tears stinging her eyes.

"Take care of yourself. And don't worry."

Harry raised her hand but Judy was gone. She sank to the bed, unsure of whether to be enraged or to cry or to be indulgent and do both at the same time. She muttered "oh shit!" and curled into a foetal position. And although she wasn't tired and she was fully dressed right down to her running shoes, she escaped into sleep.

Hell, she had already paid one nocturnal visit to the Seashore Motel, in real time, where she had an illuminating chat with Clifford Jones and got handed a suicide note that had been a millstone around her neck ever since. If she had to spend this much dream time here, maybe she should hire someone to give it a good cleaning, she thought as the dust made her sneeze three times in rapid succession. Where were her tissues? She groped through pockets but didn't find any. She sniffed audibly and sneezed.

Wake up, she told herself, but it was clear that no one was listening, so she stopped trying to rouse herself and settled into the dream, which was determined to unfold in that murderous motel. But a motel couldn't commit murder, she reminded herself, so she had better watch her grammar before the English teacher, lurking in the wings for just such an eventuality, came down hard on her for being a bad influence on her students. But wait just a minute, maybe a motel could kill; what if the roof feel in and crushed some innocent's skull? Wouldn't the motel be guilty of murder? Oh, never mind, she thought, sneezing again. No court of law would ever deliver a guilty verdict on an inanimate object, so what was the point in debating it? She had more important things to do which she might even manage to accomplish if only the fog would vacate her mind so that she could remember what they were.

She moved further into the office, curious about what was sitting on the edge of the counter, and then she smiled, almost laughed; it was a brandy snifter, and it wasn't empty. She picked it up and sniffed suspiciously, but it really was brandy. She took a sip. Velvet fire slid easily over the back of her tongue, warming her all the way down. It felt even better when she took another drink.

She carried the snifter into Gertie's apartment and sat down in Gertie's chair, which felt so warm and comfortable that she sighed.

Maybe this was going to be a good dream, she thought, turning over in bed.

She raised her glass in a salute to Gertie for her good taste in brandy and her wise choice of living room furniture, filled her mouth with brandy and then coughed. Rum! It was rum, warm, neat rum!

She retracted her prediction of a satisfactory dream; it was never going to happen, not as long as she stayed in this town.

"Dammit, Gertie!" Harry exclaimed. "Stop playing games with me!"

There was no answer.

Was this going to be one of those snifters of rum which she could never empty? Silly question, she thought with an chortle. She was dreaming, this was the Seashore Motel, and there was rum in her brandy snifter. Of course it would be bottomless. But never mind, this was interesting. Some grist for the mill, some chicken for the pot, some apple for the eye.

Harry took an exploratory swig which lowered the level in the snifter by half an inch, waited until the stinging in her throat subsided, and had another for good measure.

"Always curious, I see; I admire that in a woman."

"Gertie?"

"Who did you expect, Henry the Eighth?"

Harry snorted.

Sensing that she had an appreciative audience, Gertie continued in the same vein. "Or maybe Romeo and Juliet, Casanova, or the President of these United States?"

"What about all of them together?" Harry suggested, taking another sip of rum. She speculated about where Gertie was. She couldn't see her, but she was certainly there. Harry could feel her presence. "Where are you, Gertie? Are you going to materialize and come sit with me, or do what ever it is you do?"

"Materialization: Oh, girl, what a lovely word. But I'm afraid it's inappropriate," Gertie informed her. "It's not at all like materialization, my dear, no, not at all."

"So what's it like?" Harry asked, curious. She look around the room and got up and peered into the kitchen, but Gertie wasn't there.

"You might as well stop looking, because you're not going to find me," Gertie advised her with an amused chuckle. "And as for what it's like to be in this state, even if I knew, I wouldn't tell you," she snapped.

Harry grinned sheepishly and sat down again, unwilling to irritate Gertie further. She was certainly temperamental tonight, but then, Harry could only speculate about what it was like to be dead. She wished she could turn on the light; not that she was afraid of the dark.

"Trust me, girl, when I say that some things are beyond explanation."

"I guess you're right," Harry said.

"Don't just guess, girl; where's your gumption, your spunk?"

Harry didn't want to tell Gertie that she didn't have any. She sat quiet as a mouse and morosely sipped her rum.

"I know I'm asking a lot, Harriet. I'm asking you to suspend your disbelief in the rational, to see to the bottom of the wishing well, to follow Alice to Wonderland. Troubling, isn't it?"

Harry nodded and then said "yes," since she wasn't sure if Gertie could see her.

"You would be capable of it if only you'd let yourself be," Gertie told her. "Open your mind. Let yourself understand everything you've learned here. Your lover is well on the way, even without my learned elucidation, although I despair for Kate."

"Why?" Harry asked, and emptied her snifter, waiting for it to fill all by itself. It didn't.

"There's more in the kitchen cupboard, Harriet. But perhaps you've had enough," Gertie told her.

Harry put the snifter on the end table and folded her hands in her lap. "Why did you say that about Kate?"

"You must discover that for yourself," Gertie replied with more kindness than usual. "But I meant what I said, my dear. You have the ability to do what I wasn't capable of doing."

"Which is?"

"You must listen, Harriet," Gertie insisted. "I've repeatedly told you everything you need to know. Listen and learn. Make the connections. Realize when it's absolutely essential to reach for the stars and when it's preferable to settle for what you have. This is something which I, in the impetuous days of my youth, wasn't capable of doing. Learn to distinguish between momentary illumination and lasting contentment. I couldn't do that, either."

"Never mind," Harry said with a sigh. Perhaps Gertrude Cashin alive had made more sense than Gertrude Cashin dead. For the sake of her lovers and companions, she sincerely hoped so.

"Don't be so lazy," Gertie chuckled.

"I'm trying, what more do you want me to do?" Harry said vehemently, clinging to the ragged anticipation of waking up.

"Remember Vera," Gertie said ominously. "And remember me."

"I will," Harry assured her. With drunken clarity, she realized that Gertie was warning her. It had something to do with Vera, with how she had lost Vera. She imagined losing Judy, and ached so suddenly and so intensely with loss that it chilled the marrow of her bones and made sweat break out on her forehead and beneath her breasts. "This is awful," she cried.

"You have a choice, Harriet," Gertie's voice boomed. "You can remain detached, treat romance as a blood sport, indulge on a whim, withdraw capriciously at will. In other words, you can glide on the surface of life like a surfer on a wave. Or you can hold your breath, dive in headfirst and hope to surface before you drown. You must be true to yourself. Take me as an example. No matter how many women I chased, no matter how many women I successfully seduced, I was a one-woman woman. Perhaps you are too. Perhaps Judy isn't. That is for you to discover."

Harry understood and wished she didn't.

"I started as a disciple of love, played at being the true sycophant, and ended as I began," Gertie confided. "But then, you already know that."

"Which is better?" Harry whispered.

"Better?" Gertie said stridently. "Who said anything about better?"

"But —"

"The question is irrelevant," Gertie said relentlessly. "Better presumes that one way is morally right, the other wrong. But it isn't like that at all. No, it's much more personal than that. "

Was there really a choice, Harry wondered, slumping in her chair. Oh, but this educational process was strenuous; she was tired now, and she wanted to wake up. Instead, she asked, "Gertie, why did you disappear? And why did you decide to die when you did?"

There was a long silence, and Harry wondered Gertie had gone away.

"Is it important for you to know?" Gertie asked mildly.

"Very," Harry said emphatically.

"But it can't possibly make any difference," Gertie said.

"Not to you, maybe, but it certainly would to me," Harry replied somewhat uncharitably.

"So you *do* have some spunk," Gertie declared with a laugh. "You should use it more often. You'd be surprised what a difference it would make in your life. But believe me, Harriet, if it was important for you to know, I would have told you. And it was rather impertinent of you to ask."

Harry gulped.

"Is there something else you need to know?"

She shook her head rather vehemently.

"Are you certain?"

Another vigorous shake.

"You're lying, aren't you?"

"Are you reading my mind?" Harry asked, growing nervous. It was time to wake up, take a shower, brush her teeth, get dressed, and go to the funeral.

"You are an ambiguous creature, aren't you? Big-hearted, brave, intelligent, and yet there's a timid streak in you, just like the stripe down the back of a skunk," Gertie commented.

"Thanks a lot," Harry mumbled. If Gertie was going to insult her, she was going to have another drink.

"If you insist," Gertie said.

Harry started to get up, but an invisible force pushed her down. A warm breeze playfully ruffled her hair.

"Hey!"

"Look in your brandy snifter, silly."

Harry picked it up with a trembling hand; it was heavy, full. She lifted it to her lips and tasted rum.

"You worry too much about offending me," Gertie said. "You have to start thinking about what you want, not what everyone around you thinks is best for you."

"Yes, mom." Harry took another drink, a long one this time. Maybe she would be released from this dream if she got sick.

"You're a lot like me, Harriet. You just haven't realized it yet," Gertie said with a chuckle. "And if you're smart, you'll learn from my mistakes."

Fog rushed into the room, and Harry woke up.

16

Harry stepped into the shower stall, adjusted the taps, and stood under the hot water streaming from the shower head. She scrubbed her scalp and told herself that it had just been another dream. Vivid enough to leave the taste of rum in her mouth even after she had brushed her teeth, but a dream nonetheless. Just like the one in which Gertie had told her about Vera, the love of her life. She poured creme rinse into her hand and vigorously rubbed her hair with it. She soaped her body, and decided that it was quite unfathomable that she could dream about things which were true. She turned around and let water cascade down her back, trying to relax her muscles. She had been extraordinarily tense when she woke up, chilled but covered with sweat, her mouth sour with fear and too much alcohol.

She turned off the shower, stepped out of the tub and towelled the excess moisture from her hair. It was nearly noon. She had promised Kate that she would attend the funeral, but it didn't start until one, so she wasn't going to hurry. She was exhausted, and needed to pamper herself rather than rush through her ablations just to save a few minutes.

She used the towel to clear a circular patch in the steam on the window so she could comb her hair, and then went back into the bedroom to dress. She felt soothed by the shower and the familiar smell of her shampoo and creme rinse, more capable of facing what was to come. She wouldn't brood about the dream now, she didn't think she could stand it, not with the funeral facing her. It would be waiting should she choose to return to it, she thought ruefully.

She dressed in the most subdued outfit she had packed, but when she stared at her reflection in the mirror, it looked too casual. She was on vacation, and she hadn't packed clothes suitable for a funeral. Her pastel green pant suit would have to do. Gertie wouldn't have cared; hell, she probably wouldn't have wanted a funeral. With that thought in mind, she retrieved her room key from the dresser and left.

It was early afternoon and the clouds had cleared, leaving a sunny sky behind. It was the perfect day for a picnic on the beach or for a lazy swim in the ocean, neither of which she had managed to do since she had arrived on the Cape. Perhaps once the funeral was over she would scurry to the beach and plunge into the sea before she hurried home to Judy ...

She opened Bug and slid in, leaving the door ajar for a few minutes to permit the build-up of heat to escape, and then drove off. She become lost only once, turning right instead of left at a deserted country crossroad with no markings other than a wood cross, and then she squandered more time driving along a dirt road which meandered through the surprisingly large cemetery. She was looking for the funeral home, but there didn't appear to be one.

She spotted a group of people standing near a coffin which was hanging from ropes over a freshly dug grave. Some of them turned briefly when they heard the car approach, and she recognized Kate. She pulled in behind two other cars, got out of Bug, and approached them. Kate looked at her and nodded.

The hole was very deep. Six feet seemed a long way down. The coffin was made of knotted pine. Harry noted with relief that it was closed. The rough handles of two shovels protruded from the pile of raw earth heaped beside the grave. They looked like branchless trees which had been planted askew by someone who was drunk. Or overwhelmed with grief.

Harry's mouth was dry. She wanted to be with Kate, who was the only person she knew, but she was unable to penetrate the wall of people standing close to the grave, as if they were protecting it from the unknown. A tall woman with completely grey hair who was wearing a clerical collar under her tailored navy suit turned to face them, a book in her hand. It didn't look like the bible. She began to read from that book, something about life and death, family and friends, grace and memory, but its meaning escaped Harry, perhaps purposefully. She didn't want to know about the inevitability of death, not when Gertie's coffin was within touching distance and that gaping hole was beckoning. Better to consider death when its finality wasn't so close at hand.

The reader concluded with words meant to give comfort and hope to the survivors, and Harry's eyes filled with tears. If this had been a traditional religious service, she would have been capable of distancing herself from it, but no such luck.

"Let those who believe in life after death wish Gertie a good afterlife and reunion with her loved ones," the speaker said. "Let those who believe in rebirth of the soul pray for her swift return. And let those who believe that all is random and transient give meaning and dignity to the life of our sister Gertie by always remembering her enthusiasm, her capacity to love, the joy she brought you. Cherish your memories and live your own life to its fullest."

Grief festered and burst and Harry cried with the rest of them as two men appeared from behind a clump of trees. One of them bent beside the coffin, and as he turned the handle, it slowly sank into the grave.

"Ashes to ashes, dust to dust," murmured a tall, dark-haired woman wearing a black dress. Harry watched her scoop up a clump of earth and drop it into the grave. It hit the top of the coffin with a dull thud. The woman in the black dress was standing next to Kate, and Harry wondered if this was Gertie's niece Lila. She watched as Kate silently crumbled earth between her fingers and slowly released it, as if she was sprinkling holy water on the grave. Other women in the circle repeated this gesture in turn, some swiftly discarding clods of earth, others taking more time, making a swift last wish or saying lingering good-bye.

"Harry?" Kate said, turning to her.

She moved between Kate and the woman she supposed was Lila. The earth was wet from days of rain. Its dampness seeped into her pores and its clay-like consistency coated her fingers. She would have used it to sculpt Gertie in miniature if she had possessed the talent. She stared into the grave; fistsful of earth littered the top of the coffin. She opened her hand and the earth dropped in a lump. "Bon voyage," she whispered. "And thank you." She winced and closed her eyes when she heard it hit. Her sorrow gave great clarity to her thoughts, and she was glad she had known Gertie, however briefly.

"Lila, this is Harry," Kate was saying.

"Thank you for coming," Lila said.

Harry opened her eyes.

It should have been uncomfortable, being Kate's lover and meeting Lila like that, but it wasn't. Lila's eyes told Harry that she knew, but her muddy hand reached out for Harry's and her handshake was firm.

"I'm sorry," Harry said, and then she realized how ambiguous she sounded. Perhaps it was fitting.

Lila nodded and released her hand.

"We're having a wake back at the motel," Kate said. "I hope you can come."

"I would like to," Harry replied, looking from Kate to Lila. "If I wouldn't be out of place," she added. "I didn't know Gertie very well…"

"I'm sure she would want you to be there. She spoke of you, you see," Lila said.

"But I only met her the night she died," Harry said, confused.

"Yes," Lila said with an enigmatic smile, turning away to accept condolences from an older woman who embraced her and whispered something in her ear.

"But how could she —?"

"Beats me," Kate said lightly. "I'd better get things organized. Would you mind taking a couple people in your car? We were packed in like sardines on the drive out. And I think they want to get on with the job," she added, gesturing wearily to the two men. They had each taken a shovel from the pile of earth and were standing near the grave.

A short time later, Harry was driving Bug back to West Yarmouth. Isabelle, the woman in the clerical collar, was seated in the front seat with her, and Rachel, another older woman, was sitting in the back.

"I enjoyed what you had to say," Harry told Isabelle, wondering whether "enjoy" was the right word to use.

"Thank you. I try to make it as meaningful as possible for everyone, which, as an ordained minister of any stripe or persuasion, is not necessarily an easy thing to do these days," she replied.

"I guess not," Harry said, although this was not something she had ever spent time thinking about.

"So many lesbians have moved away from traditional religions, and for perfectly valid reasons. Although many of them are still religious, they just can't stomach the homophobia which runs rampant in most churches," Isabelle said.

"You're quite right," agreed Rachel, leaning forward. "Or the sexism. It's disgusting."

"But most people who aren't religious do experience something of the spiritual in their lives," Isabelle added. "That's what I want to address, that need for spiritual connection, whether it's with other human beings, the earth itself, or the unknown."

There was no god of mercy, no god of love, Harry thought, listening to the two older women talk. No goddess of mercy, no goddess of love, either. She was alive, she was experiencing life, whatever that was. She had only her perception of it to go by. People yearned to believe that the condition of death could also be experienced, but Harry didn't think so, her dreams of Gertie notwithstanding. What you see is what you get, she thought.

Isabelle and Rachel were still discussing spirituality, dissecting it like a dog sucking on a bone to extract the marrow. Harry's troubled mind wandered to Lila, who was certainly was attractive if you liked the sleek, mysterious type. Or perhaps that had been the black dress and the aftermath of mourning pulled tightly across the skin of her face like a veil. Still, Harry was experiencing that sense of wrongness again, of truth eluding her like nuggets of gold hidden just under the surface while she was forced to make due with a pan filled with fool's gold. Lila had said that Gertie had mentioned her, and then had bestowed on Harry an enigmatic smile before slipping away. And when Harry had expressed confusion, Kate had adroitly changed the subject. Yet Calvin had maintained that Harry had probably been the last person to see Gertie alive, so when had Gertie mentioned her to Lila? Had they spoken on the telephone after Harry left, or had Lila dropped by while Harry was out having dinner? Perhaps they had decided to have a family reunion once the prodigal aunt returned home. But why hadn't Lila said something to Calvin? And who else might have visited Gertie that night? Had Cliff Jones been there? That was one question she hadn't thought to ask him. And what about Kate? Well, why not? The more the merrier. Maybe they had a party. Hell, Gertie's apartment could have been as busy as Grand Central Station for all she knew. When had she found the time to kill herself, Harry wondered factitiously.

Why couldn't she get to the bottom of this? The meaning of what people said escaped her before she could decipher it. Sometimes she even doubted that there were any secrets or that there had been anything mysterious about Gertie's life. Or her death. If it hadn't been for the dreams, she would probably have been content to leave it be.

"Here we are," Isabelle said.

"Oh, right!" Harry muttered, making a sharp turn into the driveway of the Seashore Motel. She had been so caught up in her thoughts that she had nearly missed it.

The group at the motel was small. Kate and Lila, Isabelle and Rachel and Harry, who felt like an outsider.

"I thought more people would come," Lila remarked. She had removed her black pumps and was sitting in Gertie's chair, her legs crossed.

"Dot and Margie had to go right back to Boston for another funeral," Rachel said.

"AIDS," Isabelle added, and everyone nodded.

"They run a foster home for people with AIDS," Rachel explained to Harry.

"I suppose it doesn't matter," Lila mused, lifting her brandy snifter to her lips. "Gertie was missing for so long that a lot of people must have forgotten about her."

"One man told me how upset he was about the service," Kate said. "He said it was irreligious, disrespectful to the dead."

Isabelle sputtered.

"Pagan, I suppose," Lila remarked with a smile. "Gertie would have loved it, then."

Isabelle looked mollified.

"Would you like a drink?" Kate asked.

"Why not?" Harry replied.

"Rum and coke? Brandy?" Kate asked. "That's all there is," she said apologetically when she saw the look on Harry's face.

"Rum and coke," Harry said. She watched Kate pour rum into a tumbler and then fill it with cola. "Kate, can we talk?"

Kate glanced at her. "Now?"

Harry nodded.

"Let's get some ice," Kate said.

Harry followed her into the kitchen.

"What do you want to talk about?" Kate asked as she opened the freezer and fumbled with an ice cube tray.

"Would you please tell me what really happened?" Harry asked.

Kate dropped two ice cubes in Harry's drink and handed her the tumbler. "I don't know what you mean."

"Look me straight in the eye and say that," Harry retorted.

Kate blinked several times and then smiled.

"You can't, can you?"

"Why don't you just leave it alone? Gertie is finally at peace. Can't you stop asking questions?"

Harry sipped her drink. It was strong. "How do you think I found out about Vera?"

"Gertie told you," Kate replied, looking puzzled, then distrustful.

"No she didn't, at least not the night she died," Harry said in a low voice. "You see, I've been dreaming about Gertie, and she told me about Vera in my dreams."

"That's nonsense!" Kate exclaimed. "Look, I've got to get back to Lila."

"It's true, Kate. I also know that Vera was so terrified of being gay that she ran away to California, married a man, and never came back, leaving Gertie to run the motel by herself," Harry said swiftly, before Kate could leave the room.

Emotions flitted across Kate's face: annoyance, incredulity, apprehension. "I don't believe you," she said finally. "It's too fantastic."

"I'll mention that to Gertie the next time I have a nightmare," Harry said with a sardonic laugh.

"Gertie's dead," Kate said firmly. "She was diagnosed with breast cancer ten years ago, and it spread through her body shortly after. It was a miracle she lived as long as she did. She was ready to die when you met her, maybe that's why she made such a strong impression on you."

"That still doesn't explain why I dreamed about things which happened to her long ago," Harry insisted stubbornly.

"Maybe you just have a hyperactive imagination. Let it go, Harry," Kate said gently. "It's over."

"You mean you want it to be over," Harry said harshly. "Why didn't Lila tell the police that she was at the motel that night?"

"I knew," Kate replied calmly.

"And Calvin?"

"Harry, it's really none of your business. Now, if you'll excuse me, I'm needed in there," Kate said firmly, striding from the room.

But Gertie had made it her business, Harry thought, staring at Kate's back, watching her lean over and say something to Lila, who then glanced into the kitchen and began to speak rapidly to Kate.

"Gertie and her brandy," Rachel muttered as she walked into the kitchen.

"Yes?" Harry replied politely, craning her neck to see over Rachel's shoulder. Lila's chair was empty.

"She had this trick she used to play," Rachel reminisced as Isabelle joined them. "She would give you one of these lovely crystal brandy snifters, like the one Isabelle's holding. She must have paid a fortune for them, although she never said. Anyway, she would hover over you, filling it right from the brandy bottle, all the while making a big production about what an exquisite brandy she had discovered on her last trip to Boston. She would encourage you to take a great big sip, to make sure you got the full impact of this wonderful nectar from the gods, and when you did, you had all you could do not to spit it out, because, you see, she had replaced the brandy in the bottle with dark rum, and what you had in your mouth was this warm, harsh rum! Can you imagine?"

"No," Harry replied with a laugh, although she could imagine it quite easily. It seemed that Gertie was a practical joker beyond the grave as well.

"It got quite a laugh, although she could only get away with it with someone new," Rachel said, "and then only once."

"I had half a mind to spit it all over her smoking jacket," Isabelle said.

"But you didn't," Harry guessed, sipping her rum and coke.

"Goodness, no. You had to be a good sport about that sort of thing," Isabelle replied.

"You still do, although it doesn't arise quite so often these days," Rachel said wistfully. "Gertie was always the life of the party, you see, so pranks like that don't happen much any more." They were silent for a moment.

"I wonder where Lila and Kate have gone?" Harry asked.

"They were here just a minute ago," Isabelle said. "I'll check the bedroom."

Harry followed Isabelle and Rachel from the living room into the tiny bedroom. It was empty.

"Maybe they went for a walk," Rachel suggested.

"That's likely it," Isabelle agreed.

There was a framed photograph of two women on the dresser. "Who's this?" Harry asked, lifting it to have a closer look. It was a copy of an old print. "It's Gertie and Vera, isn't it?" she said before either Rachel or Isabelle could reply.

"Yes," Rachel nodded. "It was taken just after they bought this motel. Gertie was such a tease, such a flirt — I never thought she'd fall that hard for anyone. And she was so in love with that woman. It was such a shame when she left her. And now they're both dead."

Harry put it down. "Vera is dead too?"

"She died, what, Rachel, about five years ago?" Isabelle replied, turning to Rachel for confirmation.

"Yes, five years ago. Gertie was heartbroken, even after all those years," Rachel said.

"And then Gertie disappeared," Harry said slowly, her eyes widening.

"Why, yes," Isabelle said. "I never thought of that."

In her suicide note, Gertie had written "the time has come," but logically, that would have been five years ago, when Vera had died. She was terribly ill even then. And then she had gone on to write, "All has been resolved." What had it taken five years to resolve? "Did Vera leave her share of the motel to Gertie?" she asked.

Rachel looked at Isabelle and then shrugged. "She never said," she replied.

"It never came up," Isabelle confirmed. "Gertie never even mentioned whether Vera had made a will."

"She might not have known," Rachel added. "They were apart for many years, after all."

"Did they never see each other?" Harry asked.

"Not that we knew," Isabelle replied. "But we had our suspicions."

"All those trips to Boston," Rachel said knowingly.

"Do you think she and Vera met in Boston?" Harry asked, her heart thumping rapidly. Now she was getting somewhere.

"There was never any real proof," Rachel said.

"Although Gertie sometimes dropped hints," Isabelle added. "It was as if she could barely resist telling someone."

"And knowing Gertie the way we did, we could never understand why she didn't find someone else. She was so attractive, so vivacious, so *alive*! Women fell all over her," Rachel said.

"She did have lovers in Boston, though. Sometimes they would come here to visit her, but she discouraged too much of that. She said she didn't want anyone getting the idea that she could pack her bags and move in. But I think she did meet Vera there, and Vera swore her to secrecy," Isabelle explained.

"Her affairs with other women were just a smokescreen, then?" Harry asked.

"Oh, I wouldn't say that," Rachel replied with a surprisingly wicked smile. "Gertie was no slouch about women."

"Definitely not," Isabelle confirmed. "And why should she have spent her whole life waiting for a woman who wouldn't make a commitment to her? No, Gertie played the field all right, and made no bones about it. She wasn't one to be shy."

"That's for sure," Rachel said emphatically.

From the sound of things, Harry suspected that both of them probably had personal knowledge of Gertie's amatory skills, but she let that pass.

"We'll never know about her and Vera, though," Rachel said sadly.

"She's taken that particular secret to the grave," Isabelle agreed.

"As did Vera," Rachel added as an afterthought. "And talking about secrets, where have Lila and Kate got to?"

"Perhaps they needed to talk," Harry suggested.

"Do you think they're getting back together?" Rachel asked.

"I don't know," Harry replied. She had been so preoccupied with Gertie that she hadn't given it a second thought. "I suppose it's possible."

"That would be wonderful," Isabelle exclaimed.

"It certainly would," Rachel agreed.

Her big romance with Kate had grown flatter than a bottle of soda left uncapped, Harry thought wryly.

"My goodness, look how late it is!" Isabelle said, looking at her watch. "We'd better be going."

"Aren't you going to wait until they come back?" Harry asked.

"Oh, we never stand on ceremony. Why, we're almost like her aunts. And we plan to drop by this evening with a plate of something for Lila," Isabelle replied. "That's when she'll need some company, when it gets dark and she's alone with her memories."

"It was certainly nice meeting you," Rachel said, holding out her hand.

Harry shook it, and then Isabelle's.

"You're Kate's — Kate's —"

"Friend," Harry said swiftly.

"Ah, yes."

"From Montreal," she added.

"Kate has such interesting friends," Rachel said without innuendo.

Harry saw them out, wishing she could go with them. But she couldn't. Not yet. She might not see Kate or Lila again before she left West Yarmouth, and there were too many things she needed to know.

She went back into the living room to escape the dusty office, sat down in Gertie's chair, and finished her rum and coke. "Why did you never give me any ice, or any cola?" she said aloud.

"Who are you talking to?"

Harry dropped her empty glass on the floor.

"Did I startle you?" Lila said, bending down and carefully picking up the shards of glass before Harry could do it herself. "Yes," Harry said. She felt as breathless as if she had been hit in the solar plexus. Not that she had been expecting Gertie, but ...

"Sorry," Lila said apologetically. "I didn't mean to."

"Where's Kate?" Harry asked, rising from the chair to follow Lila into the kitchen.

"We went for a walk, but she needed a longer one than I did," Lila replied, dropping the slivers of glass into the sink. "I'll clean that up later. It'll give me something to do. Did Isabelle and Rachel go home?"

"Yes," Harry said. "They said they'd be back tonight."

"I expect they'll practically move in for the duration," Lila commented with an warm smile. "Would you like another rum and coke?"

Her rather limited experiences had left her lacking when it came to the etiquette of death, so Harry didn't know whether to accept or refuse.

"I was planning on having one myself, so why don't you join me?" Lila said, as if sensing her indecision.

"Sure," Harry said. She watched Lila put two ice cubes in a glass which she took from the cupboard over the sink, pour a generous amount of rum into the glass, and fill it with cola.

"There," she said, handing it to Harry.

"And yours?" Harry asked.

"Oh, mine is much simpler," Lila said, filling a small tumbler with rum.

"I suppose Gertie drank it like that too," Harry commented, making a face as Lila sipped warm rum.

"Yes, of course," Lila replied with a nostalgic smile. "Who do you think taught me such a peculiar habit?"

Harry thought of her dreams and was glad she had stayed. Lila provided her with a sense of continuity with Gertie, a woman she was mourning because she hadn't had the opportunity to know her long enough or well enough. She was glad that Kate wasn't there, because with her growing suspicions about the role Kate and Lila had played in Gertie's disappearance, she wasn't certain she could face Kate without being angry. Perhaps she was too gullible, but she believed that Kate should have told her the truth.

"Why don't we sit down?" Lila suggested, leading Harry into the living room.

Harry sat across from her and wondered what to say. She felt betrayed, and incapable of making conversation.

"You look rather depressed," Lila said.

"You knew where she was, didn't you?" Harry blurted.

Lila looked at her with an undecipherable expression and then glanced over her shoulder.

"You just can't leave it alone, can you?" Kate said, striding into the room. She sat on the arm of the Lila's chair and took Lila's hand in hers.

They looked like a couple, Harry thought; solid, determined, in total agreement. On this issue, at least. And their solidarity felt impenetrable.

"And you looked after her, didn't you?" Harry continued. "You made sure that she got medical care, although it would have been too risky for you to do it yourself."

Lila looked up at Kate, who shook her head.

Lila had probably used her contacts to unearth a sympathetic lesbian who was committed to helping terminally ill lesbians stay out of the hostile and often homophobic hospital environment for as long as possible, Harry thought. Someone like that would have been willing to oversee Gertie's medical treatment and keep her supplied with the medication she needed.

"And you agreed to manage the motel so that Gertie would have an income on which to live while she was in hiding," Harry continued, trying to ignore their silence, although it was making her feel unsure of herself. What if she had misread all the clues? What if she was wrong?

"I must say, Harry, that you have quite a vivid imagination," Lila said in an amused tone.

Harry's resolve shrivelled.

"I think I'll have a drink," Kate said casually.

Harry watched her lift Lila's hand to her lips and kiss the back of it.

"Gertie was secretly meeting Vera in Boston all along, wasn't she?" Harry said desperately.

"Want to give me a refill?" Lila asked, handing her empty tumbler to Kate.

This was futile. She felt like she was an unskilled amateur in the ring with two pros who were taking turns pummelling her senseless.

"Harry? Can I freshen your drink?" Kate asked politely.

"No thanks," Harry said. "I think I'd better go," she added, conceding defeat.

Neither of them protested. There were no "so soons?" or "please stay and have another." No, they wanted her gone. She rose from the chair, forced her lips into a semblance of a smile and left the room. She wished she could think of a pointed parting word or two, but her mind was blank. To add insult to injury, she sneezed the minute she entered the office.

"Harry?"

She removed her hand from the doorknob and turned.

"I'm sorry it has to end like this," Kate said.

"You lied to me, Kate," Harry said vehemently. "We were lovers, and yet you lied."

"And I suppose you were completely honest about everything," Kate retorted.

"I don't know what you're talking about," Harry replied hotly.

"All that gibberish about dreams," Kate said scornfully. "You've been up to something nefarious from the minute you got here. You should be thankful that we *were* lovers, because if we hadn't been, I might have mentioned a few things to Calvin."

Harry was stung. "How dare you!" she exclaimed. She opened the door, stepped out, and slammed it behind her. She slid into Bug and closed the door, sighing as she slumped against the seat. What a fiasco, she thought. She felt wretched. She had just accused two women in mourning of devious if not illegal behaviour. What if she had been mistaken?

And what was worse, she would never know, she thought despondently as she drove across the road to her motel.

17

Harry had been deceived. She had been cast adrift in a leaky boat, left to rot on a deserted, volcanic island. There were no trees, there was no vegetation, there weren't even any shrubs or berry bushes or ground cover, and all the fish in the surrounding ocean had been massacred by heavy metals, or perhaps exterminated by the depletion of the ozone layer. Or maybe they had been cunning enough to seek cool water too deep for ordinary mortals to dive. Perhaps they had established a secret life below the artificial lures, the nets, the skeins. Perhaps they were down there laughing and having a good time. Or doing whatever it is that fish do.

She had been deserted by Judy, Kate, Gertie, not necessarily in that order, but close. So why shouldn't she feel sorry for herself, Harry grumbled as she changed into her bathing suit and threw a towel over her shoulder. And why shouldn't she pamper herself with a little tender loving care before she pointed Bug north and drove into the unknown, exposing herself to an uncertain reception? It was high summer, the sun was shining, she was still on vacation, and by god, she was going to enjoy it in spite of everything. She and Bug were going swimming.

She stuffed her room keys into her purse and grabbed her sunglasses and car keys. She left her room and got into Bug, rolling down the windows to disperse the afternoon heat. Bug shuddered into life, and Harry drove along Route 6 until she spotted a sign directing her to the beach. She turned, followed the road to a parking lot, and fed the meter.

The beach was crowded. She found a relatively clear spot of sand, spread her towel, and sat down. The fluffy clouds which floated lazily across the sky were no match for the intensity of the afternoon sun. She felt heat prickle her skin, and realized that she hadn't thought to bring suntan lotion. She never remembered, although Judy always did.

She would find a way to make Judy happy again, she thought fiercely. She wasn't going to fail, not like Gertie did. Gertie had suffered from false pride, from a stubborn inability to compromise, to meet Vera halfway, to understand her lover's needs, her limitations. If Gertie hadn't pushed so hard, if she hadn't tried to force Vera to live with her before she was ready, perhaps Vera wouldn't have run away to California. In time, the chains of fear might have loosened, and Vera might have moved in with her. And if Gertie had attempted to accept that marriage was, in the final analysis, Vera's only protection against the stigma of lesbianism, Vera might have left her husband one day, for it was obvious that she loved Gertie. Wasn't half a loaf better than no loaf at all, at least for a while? But Gertie had been adamant, which had likely made Vera withdraw further into the safety of conformity. So what did that tell her about Judy, she wondered uncomfortably?

Harry's skin was burning. She really should have remembered to bring the suntan lotion. She turned over on her stomach and let her back fry, adding incipient skin cancer to her list of things to worry about.

Gertie and Vera. Two women who had loved each other. Gertie with her uncompromising passion and her inflexible demands, Vera with her dread of dishonour and her flight across the country into the arms of a man who could give her the respectability she so craved. Why hadn't Gertie realized that she was moving too fast, pushing too hard? Had the first sign, unremarked by Gertie, been when comfortable silences had become uncomfortable? It had happened to Harry and Judy overnight. Verbal shorthand, inevitably developed after years of being with the same person, suddenly became boring, or worse yet, annoying because it had lost its meaning. Words became fraught with innuendo, and led to misunderstandings, distrust, estrangement.

Harry could see the wrong turns which Gertie and Vera had taken. They were both innocent, for who could blame either woman for being who she was? And yet they were both guilty for not listening to each other. It was cruel, but such was life. But where were the wrong turns she and Judy had taken? She simply couldn't find any, Harry realized as she stirred restlessly and brushed an ant off her arm.

A group of teenagers dropped their towels next to Harry, promptly turned up the volume on a boom box and ran noisily to the water. Harry rolled over again and sourly inspected her reddening skin to the pounding beat of rap. She was thirsty. And hot. Fine, white particles of sand adhered to the sweaty folds of her flesh, making her want to scratch.

She rose from her towel, brushed the sand from her legs and walked to the water's edge. A wave reached shore and salt water trickled over her feet, which sank in the porous sand. She strode into the ocean, shivering at the shock of the cold water on her overheated skin. The water was frigid after all that rain, but she walked forward, intent on cleansing herself, both physically and emotionally. She plunged in and swam out past the casual bathers, then turned to face the shore. Treading water, she squinted into the sun and searched the beach for her towel. The group of teens had returned to their blankets and were huddled around the boom box like campers around a fire on a dark night.

Reassured that her beach bag was untouched, she scanned the shore, smiling wryly when she realized that she was searching for Judy. What had Gertie and Vera said to each other when they met secretly in Boston? Youthful innocence was gone forever. They must have realized it, yet they were pledged to each other through their guilt. Had they exchanged words, or merely passion? Had there been promises or only recriminations? Had they dramatically vowed eternal love and its concomitant eternal suffering, or had they reached a calmer, more acquiescent stage in their relationship? Judy had promised reunion, although she had been vague about its timing. But when it came, Harry knew that there would be no more taking things for granted.

Her muscles were cramping from the cold. She kicked to the surface and swam back to shore. The teenagers had taken their boom box and towels and had gone away. In their wake they had left candy wrappers and cigarette butts strewn in the sand. The sun was lower now, and she moved her towel a few feet away, to escape the stinking cigarette butts, and lay on her stomach.

"Harry."

She flipped over, sand flying. "Kate?"

And Lila.

"What are you doing here?"

"May we join you?" Lila asked.

Harry nodded and watched them spread their towels. Lila removed her white beach jacket and sat down. She was wearing a matching bikini which left little to the imagination. It was too bad that she wasn't in a creative mood, Harry thought. Kate slid out of her shorts and tee-shirt. Her one-piece bathing suit was black.

"You made me feel guilty," Kate said, dropping to her towel.

"It's about time," Harry replied.

"She's tough, this new-found friend of yours," Lila said to Kate, who gave her an oblique look. Lila obviously knew but didn't care that Kate and Harry had spent the night together.

"Lila and I came to the conclusion that you had the right to know," Kate said. "You hardly knew Gertie and yet you're so impassioned about her."

"It was because of the dreams," Harry replied, deciding that there was no point in being dishonest. There had been too much of that already, on all sides.

"Kate told me," Lila said. "It's hard to accept, but what you remembered happened such a long time ago that I find myself believing you. So few people knew about Gertie and Vera, and most of the lesbians and gay men who did needed anonymity in their lives and moved to the city as soon as they could. If I sound sceptical, though, it's because I don't believe in things like that."

"Me neither," Harry replied. "In the beginning I thought I was going crazy, but I've had to come to terms with it. It happened, so I have no other choice but to accept it."

"If you know so much, then, you must have guessed the rest," Lila said tensely.

"You and Kate helped Gertie disappear, didn't you?" Harry said, holding her breath as a look she was unable to interpret passed between them.

"Yes," Lila admitted with a sigh.

"I assume that was shortly after Vera died," Harry added.

"Vera didn't make a will, and Gertie was livid that her husband inherited her share of the motel," Lila said.

Harry could just imagine it. Gertie must have been mortified that she had been betrayed not once, but twice, first when Vera married and then when her husband inherited half of what she had once believed would be their salvation. The motel was to have been their livelihood, provide a reasonable excuse for living together, and give them a way of at least partially side-stepping rampant homophobia.

"Vera's husband despised Gertie. Shortly after Vera died, he called her and told her he was going to make her life miserable, just like she had made his miserable. He didn't understand that it wasn't Gertie's fault; Vera just should have never married him," Lila added.

"And once she did, she should have resisted the urge to confess," Kate added dryly.

"You mean she told her husband about Gertie?" Harry asked.

"Yes," Lila nodded.

"Twit that she was," Kate remarked.

"Now, Kate. She was obviously a very confused woman," Lila chided her gently.

"She was a twit," Kate muttered. Lila gave her a look and she shut up.

"But what could Vera's husband do to Gertie?" Harry asked.

"He couldn't force her to sell, since they each owned an equal number of shares. But he threatened to come to West Yarmouth to help with the management of the motel. Gertie said she would see him in hell first, since she thought he'd try to take over. He never did show up, but he did pressure her to make all sorts of changes. He wanted Gertie to raise the room rate, which was nonsensical, since her rates had to remain competitive. He demanded that she refurbish the furniture and put in a restaurant or snack bar. Naturally, these things were too expensive to do without taking out a loan, which Gertie didn't want to do, especially because the motel was fine as it was. The furniture was old, but it didn't need to be replaced. And as for opening a restaurant or a snack bar, West Yarmouth already had too many, and some of those were going broke. It was pure and simple harassment. He obviously wanted her spend most of her time in her lawyer's office. There are advantages and disadvantages to owning fifty percent of something, you know. It's great if you get along, but it can be a real problem if you disagree about priorities, or if one of the partners holds a grudge against the other," Lila said.

"Of course, that alone wouldn't have been enough to make Gertie do something as drastic as disappear. She would have met the bastard head on, and quite enjoyed it, I imagine," Kate continued. "But apparently he had Vera's diaries, and they were quite explicit."

"Oh, lord," Harry murmured.

"Quite," Lila agreed. "Vera fancied herself a diarist, and she had recorded everything, and I mean *everything*! How she felt when she first met Gertie, their courtship, the first time they made love, their trysts in Boston after she was married. He threatened to send excerpts to Vera's family and to the newspapers if she didn't sell out to him."

"And she didn't want to do that," Harry said.

"Not at the price he was offering," Kate replied. "He wanted it for nothing, because he was going to raze it to the ground as soon as she signed on the dotted line. He didn't care about the motel, you see. He wanted to punish her for the transgressions of his wife."

"He sounds like quite a charming fellow," Harry commented.

"Quite," Kate agreed.

"Gertie was gravely ill by then. The doctors kept giving her six months to live and six months later they would tell her the same thing. And frankly, Gertie couldn't have supported herself financially on the pittance he was offering. She wouldn't have been able to keep up her payments on her medical insurance, that's for sure. She might have died shortly after selling, but if she hadn't, she would have been in a real quandary," Lila said.

"Besides, it wasn't fair," Kate added.

"And Gertie had a strong sense of justice," Lila said. "She was furious."

"So she decided to disappear," Harry said, "and the two of you helped her."

"I tried to talk her out of it, but she was adamant," Lila said. "I was afraid she was determined enough to do it on her own, without any help, and that would have been disastrous. So I gave in."

"But what was she hoping to prove by disappearing?" Harry asked, puzzled.

"She was waiting for the old coot to die," Kate replied succinctly.

"What?" Harry exclaimed, and in spite of the gravity of the topic under discussion, she started to laugh. "Sorry," she sputtered, "but it's just like something she would do."

"I see now why she liked you," Lila said quietly.

"She said that?" Harry asked, remembering the imperious, bullying Gertie of her dreams.

"She told me that you reminded her of someone from long, long ago," Lila said.

"Who?" Harry asked.

"Her, when she was young," Lila replied.

"I'm not sure I'd take that as a compliment," Kate said lightly, flicking a tiny shell across the sand.

"Well, you're not me," Harry retorted.

"Touché," Kate said.

"So tell me the rest of the story," Harry said, ignoring Kate's chuckle.

"There's not much to tell. Vera's husband had been ill, and he eventually did die, but it took five long years, during which time he did all kinds of things to harass us. He even hired a private detective, who, luckily, was incredibly incompetent and preferred to flirt with me rather than to conduct a serious investigation," Lila said.

"I'm surprised that he didn't try to take over the management of the motel once Gertie disappeared," Harry commented.

"Years before, when she was diagnosed with cancer, Gertie made a power of attorney in my favour. It was activated when she disappeared. But you're right, he could have come east and tried to wreck the business. That was something we talked about before Gertie went into hiding, because it was a very real risk. But Gertie claimed that he was all talk and no action, and she was right," Lila answered. "He threatened to challenge my legal right to run Gertie's affairs, but my lawyer must have said something to his lawyer, because he backed off. Then he tried to blackmail me with Vera's diaries, but Gertie had been smart enough to make the power of attorney limited, so that I didn't have the right to sell the motel. He was pretty steamed up when he heard about that."

"But tell me, how did Gertie plan to deal with the police after she came out of hiding?" Harry asked.

"She was rather vague about that," Lila replied after glancing at Kate.

"She was so ill that I'm not sure she could look that far ahead," Kate said.

"She thought she might die before the occasion arose," Lila added.

Harry didn't believe it. If Gertie had taken the trouble to go into hiding, she must have been determined to outlive Vera's husband. Otherwise, why bother? But a door had been slammed in Harry's face and it wasn't difficult to determine why. "Wouldn't it have posed some problems? Wouldn't the police have questioned her about where she had been for five years?"

Lila was making tracks in the sand with her fingers; Kate was gathering tiny shells.

"Kate?" Harry said impatiently.

"It was cause for worry," Kate admitted.

"Because it could have threatened both of you professionally," Harry said.

"Well, yes," Lila replied. "Our careers could have been damaged."

Harry thought this was a bit of an understatement. Kate had been in an intolerable situation. She was a member of the police force that had received the missing person report on Gertie and had investigated her disappearance. She had known where Gertie was, but she hadn't reported this to her superiors. And Lila had informed the police that Gertie was missing even though she had known precisely where she was. Damaged? More like fired, disgraced, and perhaps hounded out of their professions for good. Making a false report to the police was serious business, as was withholding information pertinent to a case. And police officers and doctors had certain ethical standards which they were required to uphold.

"Gertie said she would handle it," Lila said.

"By killing herself," Harry remarked, feeling chilly. Had they helped her along?

"Yes," Kate replied. "She was barely alive by then, and in constant pain. Her enjoyment of life was nil. She wanted to go."

The thought that she could have been wrong hit Harry like a ton of bricks. What if they had killed Gertie and made it look like suicide? Both of them had invested so much time and energy in their careers — perhaps the threat of losing them had compelled them contemplate the unthinkable. After all, Gertie was dying. It was only a matter of time. Why should they jeopardize their careers when she could easily be given a slight nudge toward the grave? One of them was a doctor possessing the skills to do it, the other a policewoman familiar with investigative procedures. Lila would know how to kill, Kate how to disguise murder. Harry's mind curdled with denial. She had made love with Kate. And she liked Lila. The idea that they had killed Gertie was intolerable. Harry jumped to her feet. "Anyone for a swim?"

"Why not?" Kate replied rising slowly from her towel.

"I'll pass," Lila said.

Harry and Kate walked silently to the water's edge and plunged into the sea. Harry followed Kate out past the breakers, and then they stopped, treading water.

"You believe what we did was wrong, don't you?" Kate asked.

"I don't know," Harry said. "You could have got into a lot of trouble, though."

"Neither of us thought if would go on for five years," Kate said. "Even though the police investigation trailed off after a couple of months, as they usually do when there's no evidence of a crime having been committed, the stress of keeping it secret and of making sure the motel was bringing in enough cash to support Gertie became almost unbearable. Lila and I never had time for each other, and we steadily grew apart. What I told you before was partly the truth — Lila did have affairs, but it was mainly to take her mind off things. It got so that we hated the sight of each other."

"Because of the secret you shared," Harry said.

"Yes. We started to blame each other for the impossible situation we were in," Kate replied.

"I still don't understand why you thought you'd get away with it once Gertie reappeared," Harry said.

"Gertie was quite persuasive," Kate answered. "She said the bastard would pop off before long and then she could turn up and it wouldn't cause any problems. And that was true — if she had disappeared for only a couple of months. Calvin would have gone to see her, and she would have sat there in her chair drinking brandy and puffing on one of those vile things she smoked, staring him down and telling him some cock-and-bull story about some married woman she had run off with. He would have interrupted her incredible — and totally false — recitation half way through and gone back to the station to close the file."

"But he would have known how sick she was — would he have believed that she was capable of going off with a woman?" Harry asked.

"It wouldn't have mattered whether he believed it or not," Kate replied. "No crime had been committed, so he would have had to accept what she said at face value. Remember, it's not illegal to go missing."

"But being missing for five years was a different matter," Harry reminded her.

"You don't have to tell me that," Kate replied. "Let's swim. I'm getting cold."

They swam back to shore.

She should tell them about Gertie's suicide note and see how they reacted, Harry thought as they climbed the slight incline from the water line to dry sand. But then they would want her to give it to them, and they would probably destroy it whether they had killed her or not.

"How was the water?" Lila asked, sitting up and stretching.

"Fine," Kate replied.

"A little cold," Harry added, drying herself with her towel, which was a mistake. Microscopic flints of sand stuck to her and chafed her skin the moment she sat down. "Did you know that Gertie left a suicide note?" she asked casually.

"No!" Lila exclaimed. "Do you have it?"

Harry opened her mouth to reply and then saw the look on Kate's face. "You knew, didn't you Kate?" she asked swiftly, before Kate had a chance to recover.

"Where did you get it? I looked everywhere for it, but it was gone," Kate said, carefully avoiding looking at Lila.

"Cliff Jones found it when he discovered Gertie's body," Harry replied, "and then he gave it to me."

"Oh god, Kate, you didn't," Lila moaned.

"Someone had to," Kate muttered.

"But we agreed to let nature take its natural course —"

"Oh no, we didn't," Kate interrupted, her voice harsh. "*You* said we should, *I* said we shouldn't, and then you walked out on me. But I never said I wasn't going to do it."

"You damn fool!" Lila exclaimed, covering her face with her hands.

18

"**Y**ou killed her," Harry said, gasping for breath.

"What?" Kate shouted. "I did no such thing!"

"But —"

"My god, Harry, is that what you've been thinking?" Lila said, dropping her hands and wiping tears from her cheeks.

"You killed her because you were afraid you would lose your job once your involvement in her disappearance became common knowledge," Harry said rapidly.

"I don't know whether to laugh or to cry," Kate said weakly. "I *loved* Gertie; I wouldn't have harmed a hair on her head."

"It's true, Harry," Lila said.

"Well, what the hell are you talking about, then?" Harry asked vehemently.

"The wind went out of Gertie's sails once Vera's husband died. Vera was already dead, and I think once he was out of the way, she lost interest in life. She knew that the end was near, that her fight was nearly over. You know how much Gertie loved intrigue; she was never more happy than when she was in the middle of some devious bit of deviltry, so disappearing was just up her alley. I'm sure it kept her alive for much longer than she would have otherwise lived," Lila said quietly, "although I don't think she ever imagined she would have to stay hidden for five years."

"I brought her back to the Seashore Motel the day after Vera's husband died," Kate said. "She was so glad to be back — five years is a long time to be away, especially when you're seriously ill and you don't know if you'll ever see your home again."

"Was that the day I checked in?" Harry asked.

"No, it was two days before," Kate answered. "She wanted to be in familiar surroundings and to spend some time reminiscing before she died."

"And then?" Harry asked impatiently.

"Gertie asked me to give her an injection," Lila replied in a whisper. She closed her eyes and continued. "She begged me to do it, but I couldn't. I knew that she was suffering, and she believed she had the right to choose the time of her death, but I just couldn't. It would have gone against everything I believe in. It would have been like killing her."

"And you wanted her to?" Harry asked Kate.

"Yes," Kate replied reluctantly. "Harry, you weren't there. You didn't see her pain, the intolerable agony she was in most of the time. She tried to hide it, but toward the end, she couldn't. Once Vera's husband died, Gertie wanted it over with as quickly as possible. A few days at the Seashore Motel, to say good-bye to her home, and that was it. She pleaded with Lila and literally begged her to put her out of her misery, but Lila refused. I was angry. I thought Lila should do whatever Gertie wanted her to do. But now I know it would have been wrong. You can't do something which you believe is immoral or unethical. But I still don't regret what I did."

"What did you do?" Harry whispered.

"I called her doctor in Boston and told her that Gertie had misplaced her painkillers. She agreed to phone her prescription into the local pharmacy," Kate said.

"And Gertie used those pills to kill herself," Lila said.

"Yes," Kate replied.

"Oh, god," Lila muttered.

"And you helped her do it," Harry said.

"No. Gertie did it all by herself. She had everything planned. I went over to the motel early in the evening, but we kept getting interrupted. First you arrived," Kate said, smiling at Harry. "You were wet, sneezing and adorable, as Gertie said later." Harry bit back a retort; it would have been inappropriate anyway.

"I hid in the bedroom, hoping she would register you and send you on your way, but no, she invited you in for coffee and brandy," Kate said, shaking her head. "She couldn't resist, not even when she was that close to death."

"And I dropped in," Lila said.

"That was even worse," Kate admitted. "I almost lost my nerve, then. You were so sweet with her, and so conflicted. I was afraid you would guess something was up, because she didn't once ask you to change your mind and help her to die, and she'd been harping on that every time she saw you."

"I was relieved that she didn't, but I just thought that she had finally accepted my reasons for saying no," Lila said.

"And then you left. It was late, and Gertie was exhausted. She had written a short note earlier in the day, which she put on the table and asked me not to read until after her body was discovered. She poured herself a brandy, and took the pills. All of them," Kate sighed. "We talked until she got drowsy. She asked me to take care of you, to help you run the motel and deal with Vera's husband's heirs. She wanted you to buy them out, if possible. She said she didn't care if you sold the motel, but she would prefer it become a lesbian's resort. She said you could name it after her."

"Gertie's Haven," Harry said under her breath.

"Sweet revenge," Lila murmured.

"She asked me to hold her. I kept talking to her as she fell asleep. Eventually, I don't know how long it was, she stopped breathing and her hands went limp in mine," Kate said, her lips trembling. "Then I turned out the lights and went home."

The beach was nearly deserted. There were a few joggers and shell gatherers at the water's edge. A refreshingly cool breeze was blowing in from the sea. Harry looked inland at the setting sun; the horizon was scarlet, the clouds puffed up with reflected light. The sky was bright with the promise of another sunny day.

When she turned back to the others, Kate was holding Lila in her arms.

"What are you going to do now?" Kate asked.

"Go home," Harry said simply.

"You're not going to tell anyone?" she asked, her voice cracking.

"Who would I tell?"

"Calvin, for starters," Kate replied.

The sun slid behind a thick stand of trees and its rays fragmented as if they were passing through an earth-size crystal. Spray from the waves rose and danced like fireflies, and the sand gleamed like tiny bones. There was too much beauty in the world for Gertie to be missing it, too many days and nights and seasons and changing colours and friends and lovers …

"She was my *friend*," Harry said, and then she started to cry. Burnished arms encircled her. She felt warm breath on her cheek.

"We know," Lila whispered in her ear.

"I wish I had known her better," Harry said after a while, falling back with a sigh.

"Come," Lila said. "It's chilly and it will be dark soon."

Harry let herself be helped up from the sand. She stumbled behind them, tripping over gullies of sand in the deepening shadows.

"I'll drive," Kate said, taking Bug's keys from her hand.

"I'm okay," Harry assured her.

"Let her," Lila requested quietly.

Harry acquiesced. Kate slid into Bug, closed the door, and started the car.

Lila kissed Harry and then gave her a fierce hug. Her skin was warm.

"Will you be all right?" Harry asked.

"Yes. I think so. In time," Lila replied, removing her hands from Harry's waist.

"I'm glad," Harry said.

"Harry, Kate may want to stay with you tonight. It's up to you, of course, but you have my blessing," Lila said. "Not that you need it," she hastened to say.

"How can you feel like that?" Harry couldn't help asking.

"She loves me," Lila replied, and Harry could feel her smile in the dark. "What more could I ask for?"

Perfection, Harry thought. Never to be hurt, lied to, betrayed. Kate and Lila had ended their relationship because they disagreed about whether to help Gertie die. How could Lila so easily accept what Kate had done? "But who was right?" Harry cried. "You, or Kate?"

"We both were," Lila replied with a sigh. "I did what was right for me, she did what was right for her."

Harry remembered that Gertie had said something similar in one of her dreams. But that Lila could accept that there were no moral limitations in as vital a matter as life and death was more than she could comprehend. And she was in awe of Lila's ability to give Kate total freedom to be herself, warts and all. She couldn't imagine the self-reliance, the self-respect, the self-confidence which a woman would need to possess to completely relinquish control over her lover. Well, Gertie hadn't been able to do it, either, she consoled herself.

"Go on," Lila encouraged her, but gently. "And take care of yourself."

"You too," Harry said.

They kissed again and Harry walked around the car and got in.

"So did she give you any instructions?" Kate asked as she backed out.

"She said to accept your invitation," Harry replied sedately, brushing sand from her hair.

"And?"

"I haven't received one yet," Harry said.

"Do you want one?"

"Let's not play games, Kate," Harry replied.

"Can I have the suicide note?" Kate asked suddenly, braking for the stop sign and then turning onto the road.

"No," Harry said.

"Do you still think I killed her?" Kate asked quietly.

"No," Harry said, and it was the truth.

"Do you think I was wrong to get her the pills?"

"I don't know."

"Well, what would you have done? She wanted to die, Harry, she really wanted to die," Kate told her.

A horn blared behind them; they had slowed to a crawl.

"Shit," Kate muttered, pressing on the accelerator.

"I don't know what I would have done," Harry replied.

"She and I were lovers," Kate said as she turned into the driveway of the motel, giving the finger to the driver of the car which had been tailgating them.

"You and *Gertie*?" Harry gasped. This was not something she would have guessed in a million years.

"Years ago," Kate said. "Before I met Lila. She was away at medical school, and then one day she came back and Gertie introduced us. She knew we would fall in love, of course. She could have been a professional matchmaker; she had the uncanny ability to look at her friends and know who they would choose."

"I can't believe it," Harry sputtered.

"I know, you think that I was too young or that she was too old. So did I, in the beginning, but I was quickly convinced otherwise. With Gertie, it didn't matter," Kate said. "She was essentially ageless."

Harry felt envious. She wished she could have known Gertie when Gertie was a young woman. She wished she could have been one of Gertie's dalliances in Boston. She wished she could have Lila if she couldn't have her aunt. She wished she hadn't missed everything except the denouement, and then the bubble burst and she felt silly.

"Can I come in?" Kate asked.

What did she really think of Kate? Had she broken the law many times over or had she been a compassionate friend to an old lover? Had she been playing god, or had she delivered a sick woman from a certain, lingering and undignified death?

"We don't have to make love," Kate said, putting her warm hand on Harry's leg.

Like hell they didn't, Harry thought. They didn't have to breathe, either. When they had been on the beach, the attraction between the three of them had been so strong that she could almost taste it.

But enough of that. The truth was unavoidable. Kate was a cop who had broken the law. She had helped someone disappear and then withheld evidence from the police. She had obtained a prescription under false pretences, painkillers which she knew would be used to commit suicide. She was a cop who had watched someone kill herself and had said nothing to the police.

But she obviously believed that Gertie had the right to die with dignity at the time of her choosing, and that as a friend and an old lover, she had the responsibility to do what she could to help. No matter what her lover thought, no matter the consequences to her personally.

Did that make her a criminal or a hero?

Harry didn't know. Perhaps she might never know.

"Maybe you could call me a cab," Kate said, clearing her throat.

"No," Harry said softly, covering Kate's hand with her own. "Come in." She led the way.

"Let's have a drink," she said, turning to Kate, who was stripping off her bathing suit.

"Have you got anything?" Kate asked, dropping her suit on the carpet.

"I hope so," Harry replied, glancing at Kate's naked body before she turned to open the TV cabinet.

"God, the sand! It got under my bathing suit and was driving me nuts," Kate said, sitting on the edge of the bed.

Harry held up a nearly empty bottle of dark Jamaican rum. "This is all there is. Someone must have left it here." She went into the bathroom and returned with two plastic glasses. "Here," she said, giving one to Kate and then pouring two inches of rum into each glass.

"To Gertie," she said, sitting down beside Kate.

"To Gertie," Kate replied soberly. "May she rest in peace."

"Amen," Harry whispered, raising the glass to her lips. The rum was warm and harsh, but she didn't mind. She was paying homage not only to the Gertie she had met so briefly, but also — and especially — to the Gertie of her dreams. They drank in silence until their glasses were empty.

Harry's head was swimming. She was emotionally exhausted, her skin was encrusted with salt, and she wanted nothing more than to take a long, hot shower, crawl under the covers, and sleep.

"You don't know what to think, do you?" Kate said, taking the bottle from the bedside table and pouring each of them another drink.

"Perhaps even less than usual," Harry responded dryly.

"Or what it all means," Kate added.

"I think I'm going to cry," Harry warned her, feeling tears fill her eyes and threaten to overflow.

"There's nothing wrong with that," Kate assured her.

Harry fell into Kate's arms just as the first tear trickled down her face.

"It's okay," Kate crooned, rocking her.

"Damn it," Harry muttered, tightening her hold on Kate's body. She had a sudden, fierce longing to kiss her, to blot her tears on her skin, and she was glad she hadn't sent her away.

"Why don't we get your clothes off," Kate said urgently.

When she reached orgasm, she clung to Kate, whispered her name, and plunged her tongue into her mouth. She heard a muffled moan of surrender, felt the rhythmic movement of hips. She was making love with Kate who had made love with Gertie and Lila. Somehow it was like completing the circle. And god, how she loved sex, the affirmation of life it represented. The warmth generated by flesh on flesh, the wetness of sweat and body juices, the smell of desire, the sounds of passion, the pre-orgasmic tension and post-orgasmic languor.

Sex was a state of mind, she thought drowsily. Her muscles were so relaxed that they felt like jelly. And love was a state of mind. Age was a state of mind, too. She hoped she would never think she was too old for good sex like this. Curled against Kate in the sandy bed, she fell asleep.

"Finish your thought, Harriet," Gertie said.

"But we buried you this afternoon," Harry protested.

"That's no excuse," Gertie replied.

Ingrate, thought Harry. And anyway, she was going home in the morning.

Gertie laughed. "So here's a riddle to speed you on your way. If sex and love are states of mind, then what are life and death?"

"You can't trick me," Harry said, and then she laughed, hugged Gertie, gave her a wet kiss on the mouth and turned over and slept until morning without dreaming.

Then she made love with Kate again.

Over breakfast — bacon, fried eggs, brown toast, grits and coffee in a local truck stop — she made Kate a present of Gertie's suicide note. She no longer needed it, because what Gertie had given her could never be taken away.

And then she packed her suitcase, filled Bug's gas tank and headed north, toward home.

Best of gynergy books

By Word of Mouth: Lesbians Write the Erotic, *Lee Fleming (ed.).* "...contains plenty of sexy good writing and furthers the desperately needed honest discussion of what we mean by 'erotic' and by 'lesbian.'" SINISTER WISDOM   ISBN 0-921881-06-1 $10.95/ $12.95 US

Fascination and Other Bar Stories, *Jackie Manthorne.* These are satisfying stories of the rituals of seduction and sexuality. "A funny and hot collection from the smoky heart of the Montreal bar beat." SINISTER WISDOM ISBN 0-921881-16-9 $9.95

Friends I Never Knew, *Tanya Lester.* In this finely crafted novel, Tara exiles herself on a Greek island to write about five extraordinary women she has met during her years in the women's movement. And in the process, Tara unexpectedly writes her own story.   ISBN 0-921881-18-5 $10.95

Triad Moon, *Gillean Chase.* Meet Lila, Brook and Helen, three women whose bonds of love take them beyond conventional relationships. *Triad Moon* is an exhilarating read that skilfully explores past and present lives, survival from incest, and healing.   ISBN 0-921881-28-2 $9.95

Without Wings, *Jackie Manthorne.* In this collection of interwoven stories, the author of *Fascination and Other Bar Stories* moves her characters out of the bar and into life. With wry humour, Manthorne creates an eminently readable tale of lesbian life today.   ISBN 0-921881-29-0 $9.95

Woman in the Rock, *Claudia Gahlinger.* A haunting collection of stories about forgetting and remembering incest by an award-winning writer. Gahlinger's characters live near the sea and find consolation in fishing, an act that allows for the eventual, triumphant emergence of the "woman in the rock."   ISBN 0-921881-26-6 $10.95/ $9.95 US

gynergy books titles are available through quality and independent bookstores. Ask for our titles at your favourite local bookstore. Individual, prepaid orders may be sent to: **gynergy books**, P.O. Box 2023, Charlottetown, Prince Edward Island, Canada, C1A 7N7. Please add postage and handling ($2.45 for the first book and 75 cents for each additional book) to your order. Canadian residents add 7% GST to the total amount. GST registration number R104383120.